I0579619

THE WAR IS LANGUAGE

101 Short Works

By NATH JONES

LIFE LIST PRESS

CHICAGO · 2015

Life List Press
Chicago, IL

Copyright © Nath Jones, 2010
All rights reserved

No part of this book may be reproduced, scanned, or distributed in any printed or electronic form without permission in writing from the publisher, except in the case of brief quotations in critical articles or reviews.

The *Wichita Vortex Sutra* epigraph is used with expressed permission from HarperCollins and the Allen Ginsberg Project.

PUBLISHER'S NOTE
These selections are works of fiction. Names, characters, places, and incidents are either the product of the author's imagination or are used fictionally and any resemblance to actual persons, living or dead, business establishments, events, or locales is entirely coincidental

ISBN-10: 1937316122
ISBN-13: 978-1-937316-12-9

Book design by Gin Y. Havard
Author photo by Louisa Podlich
Cover image by Yulia Drozdova

Printed in the United States of America

The war is language,
            language abused
                        for Advertisement,
            language used
like magic for power on the planet.
                        —Allen Ginsberg
From "Wichita Vortex Sutra"

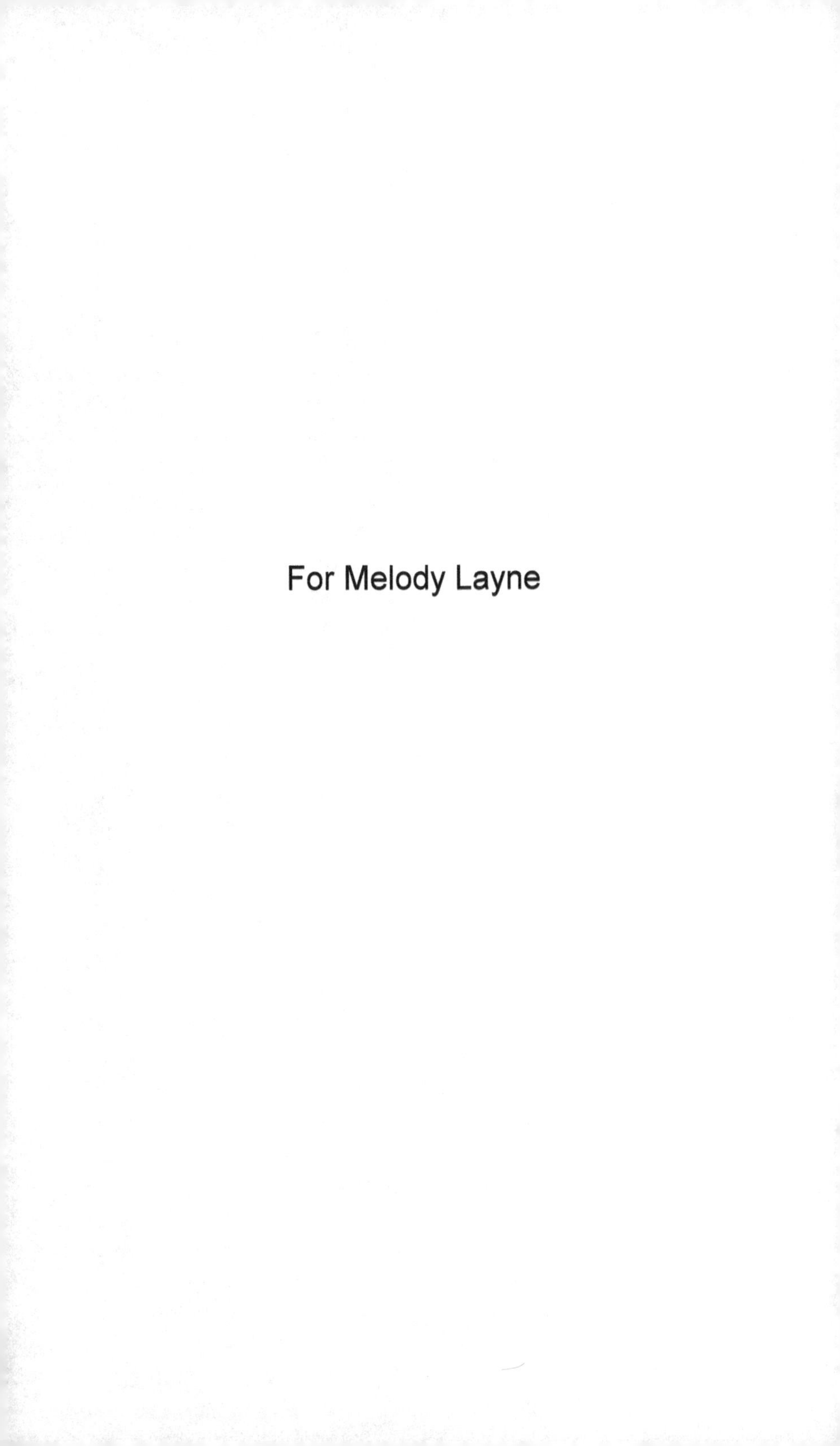

For Melody Layne

TABLE OF CONTENTS

Introduction
89 — Dead Reckoning with Azimuth (1)
1 — Fragmentation Grenade (3)
97 — Rebel (8)
53 — Worth/Worthless (10)
41 — Artist/Entrepreneur (11)
4 — Ideas, People, Things (13)
2 — An Admissions Essay (15)
3 — Labor Movement (18)
73 — Bad Person (21)
85 — Content with the Status Quo (23)
5 — Imported Silk Wedding Veil in the Kitchen Trash (25)
57 — Doc (29)
6 — Saucony After Adidas (30)
77 — Escapist Pleaser (32)
9 — Be Where (34)
40 — Action/Reaction (35)
10 — Just Your Usual Woman (37)
91 — Wasting Your Time (38)
13 — Trop Gaté (40)
8 — Debriefing (45)
14 — Blue Butterfly Falling-Out Barrette (47)
16 — Mothers of War (52)
18 — In Medias Res (54)
100 — Hysteria in the Street (59)
19 — Whimsy (61)
20 — Ablation (65)
21 — Mortifications (67)
67 — Sperm Donor (71)
22 — AT-4 (73)
23 — Cold Open (76)
25 — So They Say (79)

26 — The Hypericum (80)

47 — Man/Woman (84)

28 —The End of Grief (85)

29 — Cold Sunny Morning (86)

30 — Inquiry (87)

31 — Diary with Burning Ellipsis (88)

27 — Ladies Who Lunch on Disposable Plates (89)

32 — Laissez-Faire (91)

43 — Conservative/Liberal (93)

33 — boy, (95)

65 — Ego Confronting Mortality (97)

34 — Lunch Alone (98)

36 — Get Rich & Save the U.S. Economy in the Process! (102)

70 — Virgin/Whore (104)

12 — Ma Deuce (106)

38 — Grotto (111)

42 — Centripetal/Tangential (113)

44 — Creative/Destructive (114)

45 — Identity/Id Entity (117)

60 — Pussy/Deterrent Threat (119)

49 — Security/Insecurity (120)

17 — Carefully-placed Patterned Pavers (127)

50 — Smart/Dumb (129)

51 — Subjective/Objective (131)

7 — Commuted Fantasy (133)

52 — Tangible/Intangible (134)

94 — Stalker (136)

56 — Glory-Seeking Adulator (138)

58 — Hatemonger (139)

15 — The Dumbass Solidarity Project: A Facebook Forum (140)

90 — Cycle of Victimization (142)

59 — Detritus (144)

61 — Infantile (146)

35 — Breast Meat (148)

62 — Patriotic Anomaly (149)

63 — Wannabe (151)

54 — Hammered (152)

64 — Meaningless Existence (153)

66 — Son (155)

11 — Rubber Band Ankles (157)

68 — Doting Daddy (158)

69 — Boys Club Relic (160)

71 — Calm & Collected (161)

74 — Repressive (163)

75 — Embarrassing Evidence of Societal Entropy (165)

37 — Celebrating a 25th Anniversary (167)

76 — Overwhelmed (172)

79 — Stating the Obvious (174)

80 — Mommy Dearest (176)

81 — Slacker (177)

48 — Mother/Child (179)

82 — Judgmental (180)

24 — The Status Report (182)

72 — Bother (184)

83 — Poor Benighted Self-Centered Bitter Soul of Vengeance (185)

78 — Owner of Dynasty (186)

84 — Familial Run-in with Religious Hypocrisy (187)

86 — Should Have Gotten Knocked-Up at Fourteen (189)

87 — Book Worm (191)

39 — July Visit (193)

88 — Want (194)

46 — Love/Pity (195)

92 — Me (197)

93 — Fuck-up (198)

95 — Self-Help Nightmare (200)

96 — Heretic (202)

98 — Sit-Down Dinner (203)

99 — Altruist (205)

55 — Pothead (206)

101 — Lonely Broken Heart (208)

Acknowledgments
About the On Impulse eBook Series
About the Author

INTRODUCTION

While I was working on this book
a friend said *Quit it*. I said *No*.

89 — Dead Reckoning with Azimuth

I don't suppose you would ever believe that this entire book happens in just two minutes, with a clenching chest, sweats, and hives. But it does. It happens right there. Where? Right there in the two minutes that you absolutely must sit down in the shaded sands of North Avenue beach in Chicago. Don't collapse. That's ridiculous. And. No. Don't go over on the bench. Definitely not that bench. Why do you think no one's on it? There's something sticky there. Stop! What are you thinking? Where are you going? No. My God. Not by the water. That's almost fifty yards from here. It's much too far to cross the beach when this disoriented. Just sit down. Yes, yes, yes. Come on. At least try to be aware of where you are physically. And. So. Fine. There you go. South of Fullerton. North of the quaint brick bathrooms. You know. Quit worrying. And. I already said this whole thing happens in just two minutes. So. For a book that short, what more do you need for a setting? Time and place. That's it. That's the requirement. You're golden. You know. That's what you want. That's what you need. To know. Right? So.

Good. You know. You're not on the pavement of the lakeshore path. You're not down by the water or in anybody's way. You're not on the bench with that two-day-old sticky Popsicle residue. It's not summer but it's an abnormally hot day in spring or fall. Maybe even one of those completely freakish December days when it hits eighty degrees in the Midwest. There's a bit of shade, perhaps an opportunity to collect yourself, maybe a friend to call, maybe a few breaths to take, maybe something pleasant to look at: if it's not December then a volleyball game, a lifeguard walking back and forth with one of those rocket-shaped flotation devices with the harpoon cording, or, you know, whatever: the sky, the gulls preening on the breakwater, the pebbles in the sand, the bikers on the bike path, the joggers, the Mexican families grilling on the lawn, the black guy people-watching from the bench further down, the white guy trudging along getting back in shape after a second heart attack, the Asian woman training for another triathlon, and the parents with strollers. It's all there. Whatever you want to look at to help just calm the fuck down and stop your mind from racing.

1 — Fragmentation Grenade

It makes no sense. Nothing's to be done. How can anyone expect a contract to become a riotous nation, or, my God, a happy family?

It's absurd.

In our marriage there was no way to love anyone. We'd point at each other, or the mirror, or the floor, and, oh yes, we'd make our demands. It is no one's fault. Our me-materials could not possibly shelter anyone. Who can live huddled together under un-dovetailed illusion and unarticulated expectation? So. Fuck it. I sold the gold for scrap and decided to reassemble an M67 fragmentation grenade.

It will be an elaborate puzzle. I'll find all the pieces, unbend the mangled distortions, and put disruption back into that handheld metal orb.

Who knows how far the pieces will have gone? The M67 fragmentation grenade has a five-meter kill zone—mainly for people but animals, too—a fifteen-meter casualty radius, and a forty-five-meter blast perimeter. Pieces can be propelled up to

250 meters. But that's not the only distance those small round-torn-twist pieces can travel. I bet I'll have to go collecting all over the world. After explosions, after wars, men go home, you know. The pieces move away from detonation in pockets, in caskets, in flesh.

I suppose I could go right to war—where most fragmentation grenades explode. Or maybe the war will come to me. That'd probably be easiest. Either way, I'll definitely need to be there. Time is always a factor of accuracy. Think about paleontology. It's a miracle when they can assemble an entire skeleton because so much time has gone by, so many things could have happened to make assembly impossible. So. No. I don't want any geologic eras passing. Definitely not. I want to be there when it happens so I can just catch all the pieces of a particular fragmentation grenade.

Time is one thing, but distance is quite another problem. War draws men from the farthest reaches of the globe. It never matters how far they have to go. If there is a war, they will be there. They will make a plane, make a boat, take a tank, and go. So to reassemble this particular grenade, if I don't catch every single piece right away, if other people end up with some—like what happens with candy at a parade, disseminated, you know—

then I might have to go really far, understand the motion of front lines, and maybe learn some languages. Or something.

Beyond that I'll probably have to dig some stuff up. I'll have to exhume graves to get some of the snarled steel pieces. And that will be a problem, because out of respect I probably won't be able to dig in people's graves. It's likely to become a logistical nightmare, considering how many graves are full of pieces of grenades which would not be part of the particular grenade I'm going to reassemble. I try to block it out though I know we did try to build an us-place. Culling. Sorting. I'm unbending countless pieces of innumerable grenades, too infinite, often finding that, in the end, the piece doesn't fit anywhere in this one particular M67 fragmentation grenade.

It's a pity. Even if I can't be there right when the thing blows up, for obvious reasons related to my later interests in effective curatorship, I can surely go right to where the grenade exploded. If I'm in that five-meter kill zone, in the fifteen-meter casualty radius, in the forty-five-meter blast perimeter that's all included within the 250-meter-wide circular area where the furthest pieces can fly, I should be able to pick up all the pieces that didn't kill anyone or anything, which will be lying around. I'll bet many will be right there in the kill zone. I'm almost sure gravity plays in right from the start.

The diamond won't sell on consignment. No one can afford clarity with this recession.

So if I can't go to war, if I can't get there right away, then it may have been a long time since the grenade blew up. Except for exhuming graves, I might only have to dig a little bit. I am not really sure how deep I'll need to dig to find every one of the pieces or what to do about how they might have gone off in the tracks of shoes over the years. And. That can get even more confusing because they've already gone off, so, it's like the thing goes off, then the pieces are lying there, then people inadvertently walk over them, something gets lodged in a shoe and disappears.

That's what I mean. You know?

I don't know. I think theoretically I should be able to reassemble a particular M67 fragmentation grenade. But I guess it will be pretty hard to know exactly where a particular grenade exploded, even with the GPS these days. That's a definite issue.

Well, at least I'll be able to call up all the living people who have pieces of this grenade in them or who had pieces of this grenade in them at one time. Plenty of people were probably in that fifteen-meter casualty radius. I'll probably start with pieces from them. I should be able to narrow it down from a list from the VA or something. And I'm sure other countries have organizations similar to the VA, so I can just call them all up, or email them or whatever, ask them for a list of people with grenade pieces in them, in case this one particular M67 fragmentation grenade affected people from more than one country.

Dear Fake Advice Columnist,

I sat with my mom in the hospital. We waited for my brother's ankle to get reset. An itinerant biker was there, too. The old-fashioned kind: leather skin, blurry tattoos, raspy voice, and the kind of smile that could bite the head off a starling. He told me he was dying of cancer. Right there next to me. Right in the waiting room. Can you believe it? He said he needed to hold someone's hand. So I talked with him and held his hand. But. Me holding this gross socially-marginalized guy's hand skeeved my mother out. She took up a half-made prayer shawl, inhaled aggressively, and started counting crochet stitches through trifocals.

Dear Rebel,

I know you did your best to answer this fucking guy in his anxiety and fear, to look him right in the eye, to be present and listen. Fine. Yeah. He probably shouldn't have to face his mortal fear alone.

But your mother was right. Five minutes of hand-holding isn't nothing. You should have asked him for a hundred bucks.

53 — Worth/Worthless

The leftover people, including me, are really noncommittal. Not sticky enough for entire lifetimes. We prefer isolation over intimacy. Don't take it personally. We have other good qualities. We're just more like graphite than diamond: same chemical makeup, different structure. Not everlasting. Not harder than anything. Not incredibly valuable. Not sparkling despite included clarity. Not perfect for cutting glass. Not ever picking up the beam of a halogen light at a steak dinner and tossing it in hundreds of directions like a little left-handed disco. But. Still. As we shift and slide in our silty, slippery puffs, no one can deny we're all very good for lubricating locks.

41 — Artist/Entrepreneur

Just listen to it—that material silence—tucking you in. You're on a magic carpet under a tight sheet. Falling off updrafts causes your stomach to lurch. Air drops current and the material drifts down.

Let it drape, and with it let the wrinkles of your mind billow out from the confinement of a hot iron's steam. Here, in conscious thought resurrected from places beyond awareness, there is some mass grave of rotting dreams unclaimed. I can do nothing limitless, but I can do so many limited things. Punitive distorted ruptures will find you out if you struggle, squirm, and scream. Voodoo, crucifixion, and magicians' knives thrown along your perimeter seem quite ordinary—quite civilized. Don't flinch while a pretend body on an impossible flying machine gets tipped back on no waterboard but becomes stretched against the vertical panel of an idealized have-to-be self-perception and then push pins—these social graces, these acceptable mutilations and attacks—drive in here and there.

Wait! Stop! No! Don't allow it. Hurry. Knock that self-making-self-same-self down! Have the horizontal again and cover the decision to wait it out. Lie still under the imperative of your own have-to-breathe, even must-do, lifting under that undulating plane of bedtime percale, and extinguish any last-hope frenzy from a day of misunderstanding the unknown that surrounds you more totally than what is comprehensible. Hear prayer shouts, "Go up!" but quiet lie, and keep to it—smile your pleasant endurance if you dare such lone things.

4 — Ideas, People, Things

Michael said, "People only talk about things, ideas, and other people."

In my family we talk about nothing.

After being so thrown by Mom's misgivings, I set about the business of putting a little order in things at her place. I folded a blanket, an afghan, arranged the potted plants, and pulled the seat cushion out of an old wingback chair, one that Mom inherited when Grandma died.

A simple paper napkin, with a Bounty design, was doubled over and wedged way down in that crease where the upholstery's crafted bottom meets an unfaded portion of the well-made arm. My grandmother must have slipped the napkin down into the edge of the chair, for later, I suppose, with a sort of churlish anxiety suppressed into the smoothing down of cheap paper nothings. The napkin edges were perfectly matched, likely with all the reasons one tends never to say a word, about anything that matters, like people.

Mom's screams had dissipated in the preceding minutes. My reaction was almost gone. Who knows how many years that napkin had been in that chair? But however long it had been between there, I could almost see my grandmother's fingernails—ridged, not dainty but always properly trimmed—folding the napkin carefully. She must have done it after elevenses at ten, after those ritualistic marmalade English muffin pleasantries but before her mind's placement into the continual-drift of gray-skied coffee-cup-saucered late mornings.

In the re-equilibrated silence of my finders/keepers afternoon I curated my grandmother's inadvertent action, put the folded napkin right back where I'd found it, unnoticed and forgotten there under the seat cushion.

2 — An Admissions Essay

I am really interested in attending your university. Well. Not really. But. I have a passable—check that—I have a socially acceptable amount of interest in doing what it takes to get by. Of course I care just enough to write this the day before the deadline. Well. Okay. Fine. Two hours before the deadline.

Anyway. Steve Cohen says when writing this kind of essay, *"Whenever possible, kids should stay away from the 3-Ds—death, disease, and divorce."* I don't see why. It's like you're supposed to prove your worth and inner fortitude by talking about shit that doesn't matter at all. I mean, yes, good, great, awesome: I was captain of the lacrosse team. Who wasn't? Do you care? No.

The point is, last year, on the day that my mother and father were both killed in a head-on collision while coming home from the dissolution hearing that ended their marriage, I, having recently been informed (two hours previously) that I was now head of household, received a phone call from my extended family's internist who went into great detail about my grandmother's imminent demise.

I didn't want to step up. What the fuck? But the doctor's sense of urgency moved me, and—given the gravity of the situation—I felt strongly that Grandmother should not hear about the extremity of her diagnosis over the phone. She turns her ringer off during *Wheel of Fortune* anyway so calling her wasn't an option.

I couldn't drive over to Grandma's to inform her of the dire situation as the family car was totaled. In fact, after being described in a police report and being photographed by the insurance agent, the gruesome mangle of crunched plastic and metal was still being hosed down so it could be towed off to the junkyard after the (Awful! Pitiable! Just terrible!) wreck that killed my parents.

Usually I just let Grandma watch her shows. I don't go over there. Why would I? But. Come on. She had a right to know what I knew after the doctor told me what was going on with my family that was so quickly falling apart. So. That day, instead of forgetting about my grandmother and biding the allotted half-hour during which *Wheel of Fortune* airs, instead of chatting about the rather widespread use of inhalants, I got on my bike and headed over to her house.

I read online that, "According to a 2002 AARP report, approximately 50 percent of grandparents live more than 200 miles from their grandchildren." In our family, on average, the distance is 780 miles because there's so much circuitous evasion and avoidance between my parents' and her place. That day I settled for less than average, made a beeline on my bike, and it was closer.

By the time I got there, she was dead. I wasn't sure exactly what to do. The coroner's cell number was in my phone from the events of the morning. I sent him a text asking if he wouldn't mind to swing by, pick her up, and drop g'ma over to the funeral home, too.

It was a tough day. I'm not sure why it makes me want to go to college or why I'm sending this essay to your particular institution of exorbitantly expensive secondary education, but I guess I just feel like maybe I can hang out with the cool kids there, drink some beer, and hopefully get to use your quantum harmonic oscillator sometimes.

3 — Labor Movement

Big Business is like, "Be grateful for your paycheck. We could be in India, you know." And The People are like, "Fuck you. You're not going to India. Give us back our benefits."

Big Business is like, "The hell we won't go to India. We're already in India. We just haven't shut down our U.S. operations yet, because you're not the only patriotic ingrates."

And then The People are like, "Patriotic? How are you patriotic when you don't even ride on the fire truck down Main Street on the Fourth of July anymore? Symbolic imagery is the only thing that matters."

And then Big Business is like, "I'm the lifeblood of this economy! Why should I have to do a big charade on national holidays just to prove myself? I don't like fire trucks. They're loud. Swirling lights make me nervous. I had a bad experience at a rave once in the '90s."

So then The People say, "You expect me to feel sorry for you? Why don't you overcome your stupid irrational fears about swirling lights and get over being traumatized. It's not like that bubble only burst for you."

"That bubble? There were like three! In a row! I'm totally shell-shocked. And God knows what's about to happen with commodities. On top of that, Jesus, look at what's happening in Europe. You're one to talk about irrational fear." Big Business takes a silent non-transparent moment in the black box then comes back with, "Why do you want this job anyway? Take a risk. Figure it out for yourself like we did. We weren't always this big, you know."

The People fly into an uncontrollable tizzy. Cops get up and go to their lockers for riot gear. "A risk? Seriously? How are we gonna take a risk? We're just supposed to rail against the Man. That's you. You're the Man."

Big Business, who still hates loud noises, says, "I can force the issue if you want. You'll have no other choice."

There is a skirmish. It is unclear who might pin the other. The cops do their best/damnedest while being demonized/glorified.

After a while the two parties grow tired, bored. The People finally say, "Yeah, I guess you're right about nationalistic pride. It really is self-defeating. Fuck it. I don't really care that there are jobs I don't want because I'm not trained to do them. I short-sold my house anyway so I'm coming with you to India. But. Fuck. You'd better get me one of those hot towels from first class. Bring it back to my pre-negotiated-metasearch-OTA-cut-rate seat behind the wing where I'll be listening to electronica and breathing exhaust for the next eighteen hours straight."

73 — Bad Person

Dear Fake Advice Columnist,

I tried to talk to my mother about her life, but I didn't feel like listening. Do I have to?

Dear Bad Person,

No. And I'll tell you why. I'd much rather you help me listen to my mother. I called her up about a rhubarb cobbler. She kept going on tangents. Telling me how she planted the rhubarb too deep, how she couldn't bring the dogwood from Pittsburgh, how rhubarb doesn't grow well in the shade. I tuned in and out. Hearing only, "… and then I thought, 'Damn,' and moved it." But if you had been there you might have heard the rest.

She told me all about the new yard somewhere. I know it was the town where I was born, but otherwise I don't remember where she lived. How the sun beat down on the garden, how the limestone dust billowed over from the quarry nearby, and how she had to subdivide the rhubarb some years and double dig it every spring.

I fondly recall my mother's regaling me about oxalic acid in the leaves and how she got the rhubarb plants from the neighbor who originally wanted to kill her rhubarb in Pittsburgh. (This woman had an irrational fear of her little girls' chewing on the poisonous leaves.)

"And it thrived in the brutal Midwest sun and under the limestone dust from the quarry." Then she started on the rest of the garden. (As if I cared.) I can still hear her saying how the ageratums have taken over, but she says she's encouraging the rhubarb even though it has a new enemy down here due to the slight difference in the thermocline.

85 — Content with the Status Quo

Dear Fake Advice Columnist,

My husband is having an affair, and I'm so relieved. I was getting really bored fucking him the same way every Friday. I'm really glad someone else has to do it for a while. The problem is my friends think I should give a shit and stage some sort of intervention. I'm really not sure why. I mean he pays the utilities. Lots of times he gets milk on his way home. And it's not like she's pretty. I'm busy with the kids and exhausted. Frankly, I like watching *Law & Order* reruns in the evenings alone. Is there some way that I can just ignore this and not lose the respect of my children and friends?

Dear Content with the Status Quo,

What you need here is a lifelong state of denial. If your friends know that you know about your husband's affair, then you'll end up being peer-pressured into exhibiting the necessary moral rectitude.

Try to show up with your husband in public places where he can then slip off to the cloakroom with his lover right under your nose. When he slips away, start talking to the people in the main room about how good your husband is to you, how much he loves you, how devoted he is—shit like that.

After a while the tragedy and inherent heartbreak of the situation wherein everyone else is aware of the affair but you are projecting a sense that you are unaware to preserve and prolong your ability to watch *Law & Order* reruns may run afoul of their sense of duty. Never let this happen.

If they feel the right thing is to tell you what is going on, then you'll be right back where you started in that position of having to demonstrate a passable degree of self-respect on behalf of your children. We can't let that happen. So go ahead and let everyone hate you a little bit for no reason. Or. Better. For good reason. Be slightly irritating, fairly obnoxious, overbearing, somewhat annoying, less than courteous, and, of course, bossy. Let your entire social circle think you deserve his cheating on you. Let them think it's funny, that you're getting your just deserts. You'll never need a DVR. Good luck!

5 — Imported Silk Wedding Veil in the Kitchen Trash

Beach does not wait. On a brisk early fall day it crawls up out of Great Lake water and reaches toward Chestnut Street pulling behind it its blue train, the soaked horizon, as though a well-dressed stroll up that Magnificent Mile—lit by high-concept storefronts and LED trees—might be possible. Gorgeous, the blue roils, consuming Chicago, and then the lake demurs, receding, pulling back, and assuming again its unawareness of having reached the definition—the limit—of those trucked-in, morning-raked sands, those concrete walls committee-planned by civil engineers.

Earth slips out under those waves, hollows itself in support of them. So what if there is an end to waters? It's just perception. Not anxious only, not deferential, only, but also with respect, with propriety, with the simplicity of physics the waves pull back as much as they charge forward to claw at the skirts of the skyline. But the plan has that arm's length reach factored in. The presumption is these are big discontented waves. So if calm will not hint at all that lies sleeping under that beach's safe home sky, then where the water abuts a futile desuetude the disconcerted lake-end bashes against solidity, throws up confetti-white spray for edge-wary runners who trust in things like urban planning and put less faith in wildness.

Surge after surge the heedless lake tosses momentary veils skyward, like so much dried lavender, cloud showers for the cement cracks to catch and drain back. Those lake waters heave toward the river of headlights, while beach sand kneels in submission, in rage, in contempt, in futility outside the windows of The Drake.

The city ignores this constant body in motion, or tries to, making lists, making calls, making it home in time for dinner, making that careful thirty-five-mile-per-hour turn with forty-five-mile-per-hour braking hands at two and ten and so many offensive drivers' eyes going forward toward goals harbored with resentment, bitterness, distrust, and fear, yet, every one impossible to yield in compromise. The drivers talk, talk, talk one-sided in those hands-free-equipped cars. The words, babel chatter over songs on the radio, over baby screams from the backseat, over commuted dreams, travel as fast over unseen infrastructures as over those most concrete. Chips of cell phone conversations: *Must. Do. Get. Have to. Home. Need. Be there. You'd better. First.* And to really make the point, sometimes every single one of them says, "I'm on The Drive," which means, "You have to do what I say or I may just lose control of this vehicle, right now, and die." So swerve the talkers, driving insistent. But that lake, beach, dried lavender sky-break repetitive surging veil allows no dismissal either. You'd never recover from the guilt of not submitting to this opined whim. Even in the fastest afternoon traffic that whips around Lake Shore Drive's S-curve, during conversations where demands are made and fixations asserted willfully as irrefutable facts of what momentary existence should be, apparently a sort of convicted refusal, those thrashings of waters on the kneeling beach enter their peripheral steering awareness. But the beauty is a threat. They will die, surely, if they look long enough to perceive it.

Sun skips the lecture. The drivers are already closer to home but The Drake, the curve, the beach, the waves stay right where they are. Lest the September beach-walker be forgotten, without faith or grace someone manages an end-of-season last chance at a good weather barefoot walk. There is no Tibetan spaniel. And it's almost as if that lone individual didn't even bother to project any emotions at all upon his or her surroundings. What would be the point? Waves are water. Still. There is a smitten moment clung to and claimed able to combat winter's coming eulogies. Even though there is no real way the beach says, "Roll up your pants. Go ahead. Get in," feet are invited into the water somehow, as eyes penetrate what becomes the depths further from shore. Surface and substrate are so close to closure where the inch of weedy residue floats above the intrepid walker's wiggling toes, so curious, happy. You cannot walk to Mackinac from here. But you can take one step, maybe two, and so yes, ten too-cold bare toes wander out past the man-made world and get to that modulate edge, where sand, waves, and broken-hydrogen bonds rub up and down, back and forth, against the city's particulate air perpetually, sensually, seductively, and become waters unbound, and might stay that way, droplets forever, if not for so many rules of order. Surface tension coheres all that heave-heavy wind-wave upforce that crashes down as if to please one life.

57 — Doc

Dear Fake Advice Columnist,

Sometimes I want to be objectified by men, but I'm sort of embarrassed about it. I stand in line, in a swirling crowd, my mind sedated by the white noise of a juice blender, and I wonder: *Is there a way to be young again and reclaim my Doc Marten-wearing, angst-ridden, teenage years?*

Dear Doc,

The thing is you're an old hag. What are you doing comparing yourself to these new cocktail-dress-wearing twenty-somethings in their cute coming-of-age outfits? Don't.

6 — Saucony After Adidas

Ernestine took her pants off and sat on the foot of her bed in the lamplight staring into a brand-new running shoe. The interaction from the night before replayed in her mind. He had asked, "Do you want to fuck?" because he had to have her consent. She hadn't answered. Just went through the motions, let him get off, and got a cab. But. Holding that shoe the next day she wished she'd said, "No, I don't want to fuck. But if you can seduce me and keep a straight face about it, I'll suck your dick for the rest of your life."

She loved new running shoes. Such detail. So much careful engineering. So many design elements. Thinking of the great remnants of culture across the ages, she thought of time and this shoe. Carved alabaster? No. Great pyramids? No. Maybe the Bonneville Salt Flats.

He was like, "So you are a stuck-up bitch." She turned the shoe over. Looked at the sole. Lasting legacies and tributes to the prowess of human endeavors? Well, no. She stared into the heel cup, relishing the turquoise satin, the turquoise felt, the impressive duotone font of the decal, the recessed wording around the heel, and the bold empowered name of the shoe itself. She flipped the white leather and turquoise-detailed thing over again in her hand, felt the laces, could almost see light through several layers of synthetic mesh.

Sitting there on her bed she thought of the future—the sweat bound to escape that loose weave, grit, mud, sand, and soggy filth from inevitable puddles. He wouldn't hear her footfall against grass, asphalt, cement, even against the tops of picnic tables in desperate need of paint jobs, across hoods of cars, across marble plazas, down lakefront sidewalks and hilly rooted paths in the forest preserve.

But he might call again. Carefully, she folded back the tissue paper, placed the shoe in its box.

77 — Escapist Pleaser

Dear Fake Advice Columnist,

I mainly cave to external pressure. I like the idea of someone loving me for me, but it seems like a lot of bother to go to all that effort of disarming oneself, of recognizing the defense mechanisms, of filling in moats, coming up from dungeons, dismantling stockades, moving obstructive piles of rubble, and paving the way to my happy furry greeting card heart with something other than land mines.

I mean, no one's vulnerable anymore and having to give a shit about someone else in real ways seems so, dunno, trite, maybe? Like maybe humanity is done with love. Don't you think so? I do. It's time fear and rage have another good turn in the spotlight. You know? Power. Domination. Control. That stuff's awesome. Why disarm at all? You've got to pounce on another person and take away their sense of security and personal pride.

Humiliate them into total submission. Really show that lover who's boss.

And why not? I'd eat docile popcorn for that. But then I get super confused about how I'm supposed to have someone love me for me unconditionally or whatever. So. I guess my question is, even if I pull someone's hair and scratch up a few backs, what kind of intoxicants are most socially acceptable so I'll be able to coast through life without awareness since it's unlikely I'll have any real satisfaction, fulfillment, or happiness?

Dear Escapist Pleaser,

It depends. From your letter I can't tell if you're a man or a woman. And it matters. I know lots of women use the historically male escapes of drinking, gambling, drugs, and promiscuity. Whoopee~! They're all liberated now, you know. But there are not very many men who find relief from themselves by making their grandmother's chocolate pudding for the lady down the street when she's in hospice care for cancer of the jaw.

9 — Be Where

Be where the life runs solid—not like whey protein isolate—but where Weights and Measures get conducted through ceramic-insulated copper wire as an invalid warranty, as electric-wire arsenals carry speeds of light after the installation of 44,000-V, XLPE, CSA, and PE sheathed underground cables. Be where domestic silenced biodiesel, natural gas, clean coal, and tapped core-of-the-earth heat carries cash to dissipate fuel on a prerun accounting calendar with easygoing beta carotene repeats and sun damage specifically designed to excel what's piled up on recalibrated local roads for metadata blasting hip-flexor bronco-buck-monkey-minded citizen-athletes.

40 — Action/Reaction

Catfight: Rosie the Riveter and June Cleaver. More and more it is a woman-world I cannot grasp. Where would the wind even be? Where should I listen to clotheslined bed sheets flap-snapping dry? I run into every kind of day looking for this most-me to be, inviting implemented ideals, setting humane traps for what's best. But wherever I am, there are no catalog photos of terra-cotta tiles nor any gorgeous bare feet on warm radiant-heated kitchen floors, no little voices to overhear when it's highly inconvenient to be interrupted, no green things to fiddle with in their season.

I'm somehow crowded out. More and more the 'Merican 21st century feminine ideal relinquishes its hold—the grief of never finding her is like trying to remember eyes. Why can I not walk into her skin? How can that most domestic be most wild?

The trap is empty every time I check it. Why go looking for pelts? We are the children of the political correction. If every action has an equal and opposite reaction, is it possible to live ethically in action? It's too easy to say women still live in fear. If I win that means you lose, and so then I won't play. We are worried that our actions will have fallout and consequences, not results and fulfillment.

Light may penetrate, but we don't.

Why kill and stuff something just to have it look lifelike? The way these worlds open up it does not seem to be tragic. And yet, knowing somehow, it begins drifting slowly away. If I see a woman, fabulous woman, somewhere in my mind, and she is happy and industrious, presentations about the new economy are everywhere with cookies on three-tiered trays but I cannot see her face or walk right into her skin.

Why even catch and release? I look out a kind of window toward her, suspended by the impossibility of accessing that perfected taxidermy life.

10 — Just Your Usual Woman

There were thirteen pens in her purse; other than that, nothing worth mention, just your usual woman where rooted hydras thrash.

91 — Wasting Your Time

Dear Fake Advice Columnist,

I think about my mother sometimes. It's difficult. She's someone who did a lot for me, but, for some reason, she was always trying to get more credit than I was willing to give. You know?

I'm in this weird maternal economy. I don't quite want to call it emotional extortion. That's extreme. But. Like. I give a little credit and she wants more. So then I let a couple weeks go by and don't give her any. Run out on the rent, sort of, sometimes, too. Frankly, I'm not exactly sure what she wants credit for. I'm thinking about giving it to her anyway, just to get her crazy ass off my back. I mean, when I give a shit, I try to give her credit, but, honestly, I feel like I did most of everything myself, even if I wasn't paying for it for twenty-five years. But really, Mom didn't have much to do with the finances.

I do have some memories of her that are great. Like I remember having water tossed from a jug in the front seat onto me and my sister in the backseat at random points of family trips since there was no air-conditioning in our car. I remember three generations of our family going into high-tide water together for a silent loose-skinned dip at sunrise. And she played these sea shanties on the harmonica. So that's all really great. Not quaint. Not paper dolls and Cabbage Patch kids. Nothing girly. But stuff like laughing at bats that drop somnolent from gas-station-lawn trees and wake startled in the hundred degree dust.

We tend to laugh our asses off despite the tragic realities. And so anyway, I was thinking about calling her up and telling her about these memories that I have in some sort of verbal communication. Maybe like a story, or a conversation that includes gratitude or something. Even like do it on Mother's Day or explain the import to more people than just Mom. You know, really make her feel commended and special. Is that a good idea?

Dear Wasting Your Time,

Never mind.

13 — Trop Gaté

I rent a space in a garage a block from my building where familiar men, emigrants, take my car every night and tuck it with care into subterranean slot B-46. After the meeting but still pissed off at a colleague I thought, "What does it matter?" The garage door opened and I pulled up to the line where cars should stop. I got out and handed a tip to this new valet with the slight smile and too-young-to-have gray hair.

Women are part orchid, no matter how much we disown ourselves. I can't abide it. But, true enough, almost as if to keep my heart supple with femininity this new parking guy told me a story about him, his mother, and his ego.

Names are important. Men who park cars are in no hierarchy. David's lost weight. Fakhry is getting older and older, and I really don't know how he manages the stairs. Ribhi and I understand each other. He's a playwright, Arabic. We share cologne-drenched hugs in the middle of the night, green almonds from Jordan, classical music, and a solidarity of laughing and crying together through so many stories of his thirteen-year-old son, who slipped up and threw a brick through school windows, enraged.

It was a one-time thing. Fathers must act. But, how?

Anyway, the guys I knew weren't there that night. Weren't there to witness how incensed I was about what had happened at the meeting. I had to rein it in, be cordial to the new valet who has that gray-white hair, is smiley and pudgy, and wears those roundy-black glasses.

I didn't know this pudgy man's name. I should have.

I got out of the car, listened to the reminder chime ringing out repetitively, not for an instant letting either of us forget those keys in the ignition. The new guy said, "Is your mother still in town?" He met her on Friday. I said, "Yes. We're having breakfast in the morning."

His name tag depended from a uniform-issue band of nylon around his neck: Salman. What to do? Lately, I've felt less inclined to cross boundaries with the guys at the garage, to learn names. Being me, polite enough, and endlessly curious, somewhat resistant to discussing my mother freely, boundaries be damned, I deflected his question with one of my own. Near the open door of my silver car, I said to Salman, "How 'bout your mother?"

He said, "Oh, no. She passed away a few months ago."

Did I want to know? The ignition chime kept ringing out. I made my decision, leaned into the car, pulled out the key. Sound stopped resonating against concrete walls. So he said, "Let's see. It was 31st, August."

He revealed how everything had happened. I heard about the emergency call, the quick trip home, the sister that sat at the mother's bedside twenty-four hours a day. The coma. The tube that went into his mother's mouth and how her chest heaved on the ventilator. He said, "My sister asked her to move her foot if she understood." The foot moved.

But that was all a few days before Salman arrived at her bedside. By the time he was there, she was non-responsive. The foot could not move anymore, or didn't, or something. He doesn't know, for sure. Has to speculate.

Except. Except! Then he paused, pulled a finger across his temple, said, "I don't know the word."

I said, "Tear."

"Yes. Tear." After he had caressed his mother's hair, and held her hand, and talked to her for hours, his sister said a tear fell away from his mother's eye as he was leaving.

He said, "This is why our parents are so important to us. Especially me. Because I was *trop gaté*."

Fils a sa maman. I didn't understand. He explained in broken English, laughing at his own admission. I finally got it. "Oh. A mama's boy!"

"Yes. Trop gaté."

Trop gaté. I have to say, I thought of the man I love. He's not a man with a waxed chest popping hundreds of disco-ball cherries into drinks. Not one with wolf nipples against any of my smokey smudged luminizing eyes. He's a regular guy and with him, I didn't dare turn my synchronized-swimmer limbs into vaginal flowers. I just wandered away and wondered later if he might be a bit of a mama's boy, too, somewhere in his own lithographed cityscape. But I don't think he'd ever tell me a story standing in some garage, the way Salman stood next to my car so easily talking about his mother.

Without really wanting my mind to wander, I imagined me and the man I love leaning together against harlequin jester pillars during a charity balloon release: him with his linen newsboy cap, me with my adhesive eyelashes peeled off and temporarily stuck on a pincushion. There I was: thigh-high patent leather boots for him under Canis Major still staring down the barrel of a slosh-steaming iron that lost its UPC code and haughty purpose.

Doesn't matter. Can't. I slowed the treadle, let the pink thread run off the bobbin, zip animated through the sewing machine needle's eye, and out of my life forever. With sewing skills atrophied pieces of the material separated, slipped. The story sketchers lost their nerve.

After all that seemed wrong about perspective drawings that widen away from their closing-in focal points by putting interminable train tracks on casters—ones that just let everything splay open, regardless of any concrete sleepers—back in the reality night garage I asked the new valet, Salman, "And where did you have to go to be with her?"

I listened so hard to get my fear-rage-release wish in his answer.

He smiled a positive ribbon charge, nothing coy or inappropriate, just an electric fence in a lightning storm with subliminal flying buttresses and plenty of cleavage, not quite completely repressed with all those bedtime-lap gargoyles who surely deserved their happily-ever-afters, and their curses. Oh, sweet trop gaté. *Where was your mother 31st August?*

"Algiers."

8 — Debriefing

Every Friday before they released us to go buck wild after being oppressed all week they debriefed us. I stood at parade rest with the other soldiers. We sweated through our BDUs in the Texas heat and endured a suicide lecture.

Imagine a little, tiny, drowned-rat-looking, mustached, bourbon-skinned drill sergeant standing at the front of the company. He kicks the cement, shakes his head, paces. The rant ends with, "There's always a solution. You might not like the solution. But there's a solution."

Then, after the week's recap, he screams at all of us. "Do not trucking kill yourselves this weekend! I do not want to have to call your momma. No motel maid needs to deal with finding your head exploded in the bedsheets. And I'm not going to do the dang-blasted paperwork. So if you get any trucking ideas about breaking into the ammunition shed, or hanging yourself in a hotel room, or slitting your wrists in the shower bays, think again!

"You will be here Monday morning. You will stand up. You will be counted."

That's what he said.

14 — Blue Butterfly Falling-Out Barrette

The organ music from a tape recorder on a banged-up, cherry-veneer folding chair in the funeral parlor skips sometimes. People pretend not to notice. They don't want to upset Elise, the young wife of a man who died in a motorcycle accident six days ago. He was too young to die, too old not to know any better, etc. At the wake she stands guard by his casket, for a few last loyal hours.

Honey, we're all so sorry.

Sometimes, Elise, a mourner, or someone else obliged to be in the space to witness the effects of no real cause, looks over at the baby girl, almost a toddler now, but still with a white-ruffled diaper butt. She plays on the floor near a long-stored row of more cherry-wood-veneer folding chairs. Silken hair curls, continually escaping from a blue plastic barrette shaped like a butterfly. She doesn't have enough hair to hold it in place for long. The thing just hangs onto those few fine strands of baby hair that almost always need to be brushed again.

Her mother's pewter pin stay-twists, holds too much wool inside its clasp.

Their eyes meet.

She can stand the shock of sudden death. But not her daughter's big baby eyes. Elise begins to cry, feeling too much *nothing* and too much *all.*

Dressed-up people keep coming. Elise gets it together, holds in her emotions, does her duty. In the middle of another hug, the special pewter pin escapes from its clasp and stabs her near a clavicle. She jumps back from the unintended consequence of the embrace and manages to reclose the pin with blind fingers below a strained bent-to-see-something-so-close neck. She does her best. The pin hangs then, slanted, on a pinched lapel. *That's lovely,* someone says, not quite to point out the pin's haphazard arrangement, worse than before.

Elise thinks of stolen future days, begins to cry, again. The person who hugged her, who made the pin stab her, leaves, the obligation having been met. Elise cannot get it together this time. Tears flow. Friends shuffle, look away, disperse.

An older man stares at her from a far corner, then catches himself in the fixation, goes out the side door to have a cigarette, even though he shouldn't. He should want to quit.

Inside still the white-ruffled diaper butt, patent leather shoes, and blue butterfly falling-out barrette come crawling out with their toddler curls from under a wooden folding chair missing some veneer. A nearby ancient matron's voice says, *Why. There you are!*

Not wanting to understand quite so very much from that tone of voice the white-ruffled diaper butt moves back under the row of wooden folding chairs. Back away from the *Why. There you are!* ancient lady, who—after a despairing minute after accosting such a shy child—falls asleep, doesn't notice three little fingers working their slow, curious way into the brass-hinged pinch point.

Elise stops shuddering convulsively when her mother takes her elbow and whispers. The sequence repeats. The pewter pin on Elise's lapel pops open again. Instead of allowing it to stab her this time, having adapted, Elise hears the little rotating clasp click over, feels the pin loosen, steps back from the three-hundredth hug. She lets the pin fall, lost.

Instinctively Elise's eyes travel to the floor, demanding to find the pewter gift with all its significance among the weeds in the ornate carpet garden. Unnecessarily, several men—old and young, all hovering, useless—leap to action: leaning over, each hoping to be the one to pick up the precious pin, to offer it back, to be helpful, to do something other than flirt with the floor.

Still snoozing, the *Why. There you are!* ancient lady amply shifts in her seat.

Three fingers, baby girl almost-a-toddler-now fingers, twist and pop. Soft bloody broken bones get crushed somewhere inside the chair.

Why. There you are! dozing wakes startled, reacts haphazardly to the wailing scream of the child underneath her in agony and so changes instantly to, *Oh my dear Lord in Heaven. I didn't know you were down there, Sweet Pea. Dear Heavens. Oh no. Oh God. Don't cry, precious girl. I didn't mean to. I am so sorry.*

Hugging no one in that moment, unwilling really, Elise moves away from her post near the casket, walks over to her child in another slow-motion refusal to panic, picks the little girl up ruffled behind and all, and lets her bleed onto the best white silk blouse she's ever owned for two days.

Red face screams over a shoulder as the pace picks up and the young mother hurries down the aisle of chairs, through the door, across the patchy August grass to her car, and all the way to the county's emergency room.

What can anyone do?

At the funeral home people disperse as quickly as is appropriate, which is unclear. The old woman who was in the chair is a wreck. She gets comforted by Elise's mother, who hates her, always has. Even they go, individually, after a while.

The flowers stay.

The last person, an older man, not a great-uncle, but someone who would have probably stopped over to the house anyway, picks up the blue butterfly barrette. He thumbs it open, feels its tiny open-hinged plastic bed of nails, clasps the thing tight again, and drops it, already forgotten, into his pocket.

16 — Mothers of War

An anarchist sat on my lap screaming, "Why?"

I said, "Hush, little baby, don't say a word. Mama's gonna buy you a mockingbird."

The anarchist threw the very thought on the floor saying, "I don't care. I don't want it."

I said, "Fine. Have it your way," and watched her throw my refusal against the table leg with her own. Without caring, without wanting anything, we both let willingness break into three irreconcilable pieces.

And then she blamed me, for everything. Began with her agony. Wretched momentary girl.

I said nothing. Could not bear the responsibility bouncing on my knee, but a patrolling Marine lit a sleep-deprivation cigarette between us. Her crying stopped. I felt less infringed upon for a moment but then, remembering that he was really trying to quit smoking, the Marine put the burning thing down after drawing one long last breath. The anarchist went to her crib for a nap and the Marine extinguished that single cigarette—more fragile than most gods—somewhere not that important near the bounds of freedom.

53

18 — In Medias Res

For instance, there is a child crying in the back of a classroom. This is not the child of any madonna. This is a regular kid, kind of a stupid one without a lot of opportunity. He does not raise his hand. And he might not even be a boy.

Regardless, he is unseen.

Don't get all freaked out. I'm not hallucinating. He's not a ghost, goblin, or angel. He's just an idea. He's that theoretical conception of unfulfilled potential. He is no real human fruition—a pedagogical apparition of twining potential and incapacity, unteachable.

This child though—this idea crying in the back of the room—really is an unbearable nuisance. He seems to alight, and finds himself on the ceiling tile, near the computerized projector, bumps up against that 2,000 ANSI Lumen beam of tricolor light—blue, green, red—and then sweeps down, screeching as loudly as any silence ever can.

He lands on the fold of my ear and says, "Are you sure? You should probably be more certain."

I swat him away. Stupid idea.

But he will not go away. He insists. "What do you know? Only people who know what they're doing should teach. You don't have any business here. Why even bother?"

I do not dicker with him. He is right as much as he is disruptive. I have no clue what I'm doing. I hate that he inhabits that room, haunts it, so I do everything I can to be ready, to have prepared myself for anything before ever stepping foot into his domain. I carry books, notepads, red pens, gold stars, scratch paper, dry erase markers, and an attendance sheet.

He is not listed. He goes back to the ceiling. I do not call his name.

I will not be manipulated.

I'm new to teaching and not quite used to dealing with the tangible and intangible forces of classroom respect. Yet I will not allow someone beyond the pale to taunt me with such discourteous insistence to malign my efforts. The twelve real students are staring at me, expectant, for the better part of two hours. I suppose I could ask them to quit it, to stop looking at me, to leave me alone, but it might not be appropriate, given the circumstances.

I do not care that he is that pitiable child of whom the state and church can never quite rid themselves. He is the one for whom no one cares quite enough. The one no one believes in. A child ever exempted from his own requisite rescue. What's expected of him but to falter, to fail? But. Fuck it. What can I do about it? Let him sit there on the ceiling, watching. The reality of class goes on.

When I'm in the room, teaching in reality, I try not to concentrate on him, because he is completely absurd. He swoops and dives so close to me that his passing sends quivering trembles through my body, yet I do not address him directly. I ignore him, feeling that he must be at least as afraid of me as I am of him. I refuse his possession of my mind; I concentrate on the other twelve people in the room.

Most of this has no bearing. The point is, there probably is no unseen problematic child of behavioral pathology screaming and crying and using God knows what other psychological intimidation tactics on me from up there on the ceiling. That's just some stupid idea. I'm really the teacher and, even if I'm the kind of ninny who frets about the implications that hovering ideas actually do have, I am deserving of respect.

He offers none.

But how absurd are our expectations of this child on the ceiling? What valiant anti-antiestablishment establishment fight is bred in him?

When he draws you in, there you are bumping your own head against the projector, looking down on a room full of hopeless earnest fools eager to learn something about anything, and you find yourself having to resist the domination of your own mind by his entrenched apathy.

Why resist? Why not submit? Why not go along with it? Why not let an ignorant child tell you exactly how it is and how it's going to be?

Why not enter into alliance with this child, this stupid idea?

Shouldn't he fight to become some kind of self-possessed self-respecting something in reality? Empowered! No. Probably not. I forgot. The assumption is not that he won't. It's that he can't. Beyond that, he has no voice. He's silenced by nonexistence but also by the bell curve's adamant case that he does. So damned by pedagogical theory, he is forced, forever, to never learn.

The reality is, we are in the classroom, right now. Mainly, we are here because we all want to write as well as we can. I say things like, "What was that book you recommended, Jim?" Or, "How is it that a canoe trip is like a marriage, Lotti?" Knowledge is no beacon. But we laugh, together, which makes that idea, that stupid irascible disconsolate unaware unteachable child, dissipate altogether.

100 — Hysteria in the Street

Dear Fake Advice Columnist,

I am divorced. I really loved my husband, but I was a bitch and he was an asshole. I've got proof. I flipped channels when that plane landed on the Hudson.

Dear Hysteria in the Street,

Oh my God. You are a bitch. Totally. You are a train wreck, and everyone knows it. People are talking about you. And not even behind your back. They are talking about you to you, and everyone thinks you need help. So I guess you might just get a job as a cashier somewhere. There are a lot of such jobs. People take your money at a lot of different businesses. But remember, you can't flinch. You cannot react at all when mothers with enormous tits come in buck naked under lavender bathrobes demanding, "My son needs his Sunkist soda before school. He's in the car." You cannot flinch when old Indian women show you their ripped-out linings of their purses. It wouldn't be polite.

Cashier jobs are great. You can even put your own money in your cash register sometimes. Just don't take any back out.

19 — Whimsy

Anyway, Milo decides we should crawl up the bar, over the curling roses in the woodwork, under that old blower they use to keep the smoke inhalation to a minimum, and just go right smack into the mirror.

It's an antique. I admit a fleeting moment of reservation. We'd been enjoying ourselves, chatting it up with an irascible sushi chef and the bartender. Not that one girl with curly hair but the skinny guy in belted black jeans. The one who always makes us listen to Kenny G. on Tuesday nights.

Conversation was enough for me. I didn't need the escalation but Milo seemed to know best.

Bitter glee, so unburdened by the fates as to seem almost, well, almost as if our youth did exist, replaced any notice of the passing time. So it didn't really matter that I was afraid. Milo climbed into the mirror demanding that I follow.

I don't blame him for not explaining more. Likely he didn't know what either of us was about to get into, couldn't have foreseen. But he seemed so experienced that he might have mentioned what would happen when our dives began.

Although, really, I forget myself and am not sure I can describe it all that well, not from the very beginning. Glass is an amorphous solid, a sort of impossible-to-perceive liquid. I believed it wasn't substantial. Still I didn't know how fast, or how slowly, how thick or thin, how sick or healthily I would have to go on to move through such a strange seemingly-solid fluidity.

Oh. Wait. Now I remember Milo saying that diving down into the mirror felt like rolling through a roundness, hard and unfathomable, and it would almost be like sliding around the curve of one of those colored twists that stays, forever trapped, in a marble.

We each had our individual experiences but falling through the mirror happened to both of us simultaneously. There was no fun house displacement or condensation. He was not me; I was not him. We were one with the reflection.

Marbles don't shatter. They bounce and clatter. That's the kind of place it was. The world inside the mirror isn't really that different from a lakeside walk. It is darker, sure. But not all completely unfamiliar. It's not what I expected which was an underground mine that opens out like a tree fort made out of peaty stuff and branches into civic-planning-committee train stations on a mythological river, you know? Or an igloo. Or, no!, a cave, where water drips stalactite-ish, into calcified blue, artificially-lit pools of well-marketed discovery. And it's not hot, either. I'm not sure what it's like exactly. You'll have to ask Milo.

But however it was there was no oxygen, so at one point, with self-preservation in mind, we decided to just give up breathing, to conserve what reserves we each had packed away deep down in the alveolar recesses of all the amorphous impossibility inside ourselves. (That was my idea.) After a while we wanted so very much to begin again with our lives the way they had been that we tumbled so sleepily, like zoo-kept belugas, against our window of the world. You know the one. It's like the one at Rockefeller Center, only bigger. Like, Grand Canyon big, only glass.

I huddled with the masses. He nuzzled like a baby calf, only tougher, more respectable.

When we woke (and don't ask me what exactly happened, because I don't remember everything and—thank God—neither does he) there was something different. I felt sort of crowded in a way that I didn't know before. I stood up but found no internal way back out and up through the liquid marble twist. We'd held off for a long time but used up our reserves. Breathing became necessary. I had to inhale something, didn't I? So I just took my surroundings in. It wasn't agony when I felt that marble twist fill my lungs. It was like lavender ornamental florist beads that put attractive weight in the bottom of a minimalist crystal vase to hold the flower stems just so.

I was completely committed. My chest filled with the weight.

I had been in love, twice, but had never been possessed to the point that I required exorcism. So, it was very odd to realize, to know, to become aware that we were the same human being, suddenly. It was all elbows and squished in.

We denied its influence, its very reality. There is something so unnecessary about a friend who actually lives in your entirety. Like a lifetime witness. I like Milo, don't get me wrong. And, to my knowledge, Milo's never once said a bad word about me. It is what it is, I guess. Just too much, too close.

So anyway, I stood there—right there with him—trying to accept that we'd become one being breathing twisted glass lung-filled something against our reversing image window of the world into and through all the me of him that I never even tried to get used to.

20 — Ablation

He didn't want to know what would happen at all in the next two hours and wished he hadn't been told. Ray Hollowell let the word play over and over again in his mid-mind, a place where metamorphosis means nothing. "Ablation," the doctor had said again right when Ray arrived with his wife at the cath lab that morning.

Ray didn't mind the upcoming procedure. He understood necessity, survival. But being unconscious bothered him. The orderlies might accidentally let him slide off the gurney and onto the floor—it could happen when they were shifting him onto his bed in recovery. He put it out of his mind.

Ray lay there, staring at the TV, trying not to look at the dirty vent in the ceiling, trying not to think about sliding off the gurney while unconscious, trying not to think about the short-circuit rhythm of his heart, or about how any tiny wires were going to go in through a vein in his neck, or the way electrodes mapping the impulses of the muscle in his heart worked, or how on earth they managed to weld-kill the place where irregular beats began to cause such erratic disruption.

Ray thought someone should probably come clean the vents. Didn't seem right for the vent to be dirty in a hospital. But he didn't call the nurses' station. Figured he'd maybe mention it after the procedure. Wouldn't want to tick anyone off before he went under anesthesia and couldn't defend himself in a potential fall.

21 — Mortifications

Sometimes I sit here and think of different ways to pass time. I reorganize shelves when they are not pleasing. Maybe they are crowded or cluttered somehow. I like them to have a certain order. And sometimes I change my mind about that certainty. This usually depends on the season.

Like now, in the winter, I can put the beach towels and the camp chair—the black one I bought my father for Father's Day the last year he was alive—further back since I don't really need ready access to them. I put my summer clothes away also so I can make more room for sweaters. I also reorganize if things keep falling down from the shelf or tipping over on the shelf. I have several kinds of shelves even though this is a rather small apartment—it's a studio. I have the shelves in the kitchen—in the cabinets. There are about fifteen shelves in the kitchen. And I put a little shelf over the sink so that is another shelf. These shelves are very important. It is important that they are always organized—making food is about awareness. There needs to be awareness about the inventory of food and spices which are available for making food and awareness about the tools required for cooking. So having a mental image of your shelves is very important. These shelves are my highest priority.

I have a few shelves which are ancillary to the kitchen and cooking. These are the top of the refrigerator, the shelf of cookbooks which is actually in my living area, and the oak armoire (given to me by my mother on my sweet sixteen) which now serves as a pantry. I have lots of bookshelves but they almost never get rearranged. I have one area for reference books, one area for books of poetry, one area for children's books, one area for field guides, one area for books about money, one area for what I consider to be highbrow reading, another area which I consider less highbrow, and several miscellaneous shelves that are arranged more or less aesthetically.

The shelf I rearrange most often is above my bed. I rearrange it when I need to store something or when I've forgotten exactly what's up there. I keep a few nice things in case I ever buy a house. I have a set of silver candlesticks from the 1870s up there. I thought about getting them down at Thanksgiving when my mother and sister came. But it seemed discordant. I hadn't really pictured my silver candlesticks on a secondhand coffee table. I hadn't pictured me sitting on the floor, my mother in a free rocking chair I found on the street in

Philadelphia, and my sister in the desk chair—giving thanks. There wouldn't have been room on the table anyway. I'll get them out next year maybe. Or take them to wherever I'm going.

I also put a lot of time into decorating my apartment. I decided to put up some pictures of people who make me happy. So I've got some pictures on the walls. There is an area to sit down and talk. There is an area to watch television. And I bought a used electric piano where I play hymns and folk songs when I get so bored with the silence. I guess I forgot to mention that there is a shelf with some piano music on it when I was telling about the shelves before.

If there's no shelf on which to work, I'll get up and make tea. Most days I watch at least one movie. Depending on the movie I end up thinking about someone I know, someone the movie reminds me of or who I think might like that same movie. Sometimes I go so far as to mention it the next time I see that person or if they live really far away I just send them an email about it. If it's not nighttime (which is when I watch movies) I read something, maybe from a magazine or a biography or a book about finance or perennials to put in the garden or something a friend recommended months ago. I rarely finish reading anything.

I don't always finish dealing with my shelves, either. There is a shelf above my coatrack that I have decided to ignore for the time being. There are two boxes on that shelf. They hold paperwork that extends back into all my identities and addresses and lives and roles and I just can't rectify those boxes right now—so I leave that shelf alone.

67 — Sperm Donor

Dear Fake Advice Columnist,

My wife recently had a baby. Or she is thinking about having a baby. Or she is thinking about getting me to marry her so she can have a baby. Or she is thinking about fucking me once after we stumble home from the bar drunk so she can have a baby. Or something. I can't really figure it out. Is there any way that I can tell if I want to have a baby with her?

Dear Sperm Donor,

Whoever this woman is, she is crazy. She obviously wants nothing substantial with you, and you don't deserve to be treated like that, so dismissively. It's demeaning. Hard to say what any of us wants, so I'm not sure if you'll ever figure out whether you want to have a baby with her. But you should probably fuck her, and figure it out later.

22 — AT-4

Have you ever picked up an AT-4? That is a serious weapon. You have to be pretty pissed off to come anywhere near that thing. But I did. It intrigued me. I was an E-2. An army private going through the motions. I was being trained. They call it soldierized. I had signed a contract. Whatever the justification, on a quiet morning out under the smudged skies over the Ozarks, I picked up that AT-4. And I shot tracer rounds right into that bastard horizon.

It was nothing to consent to this act. Much less a commitment than volunteering to kill and be killed. I remember picking up the weapon and almost laughing at it. The AT-4 is nothing. It's basically a piece of PVC pipe, plastic. Made to be light, easy to carry. The thing almost seems silly. If you drop it on the ground it makes this *donk* sound.

But then when you shoot it, there's that enormous back-blast.

What submissive hell do we ask of others? In the living room, where children grow and where we daily assault our loved ones, in the workplace where we exert our authority as a matter of course, on the battlefield where we are so excited to get to kill and be killed, what are the motions we're asked to go through?

If Mom or Dad yelled at each other it's a pattern. Easy to pick up as an AT-4. Why are patterns of anger so hard to put down?

What if no one is asking you to shoot? What if no one needs you to be as pissed off as you are? To keep you identified with such rage? If it didn't define you, would you still choose it?

As you dismantle the defenses the vulnerability mushrooms. Hard, though. Really hard to let the rage go. The definition of who you are becomes less clear. The integrity goes. And if there is a sense of vulnerability, if there's no integrity, of dissolution even, why not indulge in an Ozark afternoon of assault with an antitank weapon?

Why do we ask boys, and a few little girls, to keep rubbing salt in the wounds of personal trauma? Why do we clap for the man with the AT-4? Why don't we say, "Hey! That shit is crazy! Put that thing down! You're gonna hurt yourself!! You'll put someone's eye out!"

Our military force is a volunteer army. I suppose it's better than a draft. We don't want anyone going off to war who doesn't really want to be there. Yet, isn't there a problem sending those who can't wait to go? Every kid who joins—we were almost all kids—is just a little too angry. Willing to shoot holes in every edge and horizon. Willing to die for any good reason. Sometimes for none.

The world asks just a little too much of that pissed-off kid. He's making no sacrifice. He's doing no duty. He is killing himself on behalf of the world. He is acting out, might only need Ritalin, if we didn't need an army.

23 — Cold Open

I jumped up, rushed to the front of the classroom, grabbed the green pen, and wrote on the whiteboard. "Nobody like me would go on a trip like that." It was all there: her whole story. But it only existed in her mind, not on the page.

She felt it was all there but, for us, there was nothing. No desperadoes, no too-tender thrust-back expediency, no fortune-telling short haircut with a diet cream soda while spinning pottery, no embalmed twelve-year-old angels.

So I asked, "Who is nobody?" She looked at me, dumbfounded, stunned, with a smirk that said silently, "Well, you know exactly who 'nobody' is."

And yes, I suppose I'm judgmental enough and can make the right assumptions. I knew her so I saw him, her nobody. He was slouched, roaring, strange, original, expectant, with tendinous hands in his pockets, a beard full of late-night jazz, a ringleader on his way to Gooseberry Falls out on the North Shore leaving Duluth, and yet always there he was as a rapid inhospitable fan party rig at the flower market.

What else could I do? I had to take a stand. I filled in no blanks with what was implied and insisted she tell me the specifics of the story in her head. "Who is nobody?" I didn't want to force her to define, to describe, and explain. But she had to. She said, "Family, friends." Okay. I said, "What is 'like me'?" Again, she didn't get it. Wasn't it obvious? Didn't I just know by looking at her? Beautifully, dramatically, she tossed arthritic liver-spotted hands around. Perhaps she'd been a dancer but I didn't know, just waited, listening. And there it was, her answer: "Well, I was eighteen, in college, had just gotten married, and it was 1956."

So. I was wrong. There was nobody at a flower market.

I kept pushing. "What is a 'trip like that'?" She got frustrated, became irritated by my pressure. "There were no roads. It was just jungle. My mother must have been scared to death but never said a word. And there was a coup as soon as we crossed a border."

Ah, yes! Beards full of jazz. Tremendous. Having written most of this on the board, I was able to show how a piece of nonfiction can be built by moving beyond the ego-based assumption of a person right in front of you and toward a shared understanding that can stand on its own, offering itself up from the page without any storyteller present.

Give me a quilted flint and jaw. Some impossibility like harmless rooms. A leaking pipe. Let me touch that week-old beard by reaching for the sound of it.

We coupled her initial generalization to a more detailed description that rooted her reader in the scene, the time, and did pretty well to really set the stakes for a trajectory in her piece. The first sentence of her nascent essay called out to readers: *Nobody like me would go on a trip like that.* The next sentence was straight from the vat of grapes I jumped into with my bloomers pulled up and my skirts tied high around my waist. It was a sentence built of her own frustration. When given to me all the words were offhand, dismissive, caustic, and explanatory. But when left for the reader, they were finally enough. Thank God for the words. Even if only offered at my insistence and extracted by my prodding, because there it was now and so easily it moved the reader on with, "My friends and family certainly hadn't expected an eighteen-year-old girl, in college, would do such a thing, would drive so far— all the way from New York City to Chile. Certainly not me after just getting married, before I ever had a real shot at medical school."

25 — So They Say

Why introduce yourself with some conversational imperative like, "You know how it is."? So push, push, push on generations. In whatever mirror presents itself, there is a surfacing from endless me-too Mom-comparison. Listen. "Yes. Yes, so they say." Look. Aimless amidst the uniformity. Eyes adjust like they do in the night and linger on the variations: the tall girl's insurmountable fear, the old woman's impossibly hopeful laughter. Over there! Her eyes are blue and hers are sleepy from exhaustion, and there! Look, not into them, but at another pair haunted by muzzled memory. Isn't it something how that one moves? Play by play and play by the rules, girl. Remember self-sacrificial things like, "No, please, you go ahead," wearing blank name tags. Finally you see how it will be for you in this newest Woman, how you will terminate frustration long enough to wear the flattery, finery, and suffocation of cast-off hand-me-down corsets.

26 — The Hypericum

Come to my father's funeral! Why? Why not? Come for the music, the hypericum, the pencil sketch of the young owl balanced on its easel, the crisp fall day, the friends, the family, and to see the borrowed pall over that cherry casket. Oh, come on. It'll be wonderful. There's so much to see, to do. So many people to meet, to know. Well. Except my father. You can't meet him anymore, can't know him anymore. But. Aside from him, you can meet almost anyone he really knew well.

At the wake the night before, come here. Look: at my mother standing near his corpse talking to some neighbors we've known for years. Mom, a biologist same as Dad, explains how my father studied the immunologic function of green-boned tree frogs. Listen! Do you hear her? She's saying how they collected frogs in the swamps of Suriname. He needed them for his research, his doctoral dissertation all about pigmentation. So then hear her tell how pleased he would have been, how much he would have appreciated the shade of cantaloupe green he turned when he died.

Listen with our old neighbors as Mom explains how red blood cells rupture when they are no longer oxygenated. She'll tell you how it is, how constant the processes are. Rupture normally happens to red blood cells every few days—nothing lasts forever. When you're living, alive, vibrant, vigorous, hungry, and tired, the cells never rupture all at once for that lack of O_2. Day-to-day the liver tidies up, takes care of it, handles everything without being asked, clears out the goners. Mom keeps explaining it to our old neighbors: only at the end of life does biliverdin really have a chance at pigmentation. "So he turned the most beautiful green." Fascinating. To her. To us? You? Are you terrified with the neighbors? I think maybe you are. So I walk up very slowly, fingers intertwined, but loose. I separate my hands, place one on my mother's shoulder, and one on the arm of our nearest old sweet neighbor. I say, "Thank you so much for coming." And then I stand there with my mother. There is nothing left to do that night at the wake, except—Come with me! We'll slip into the banner room the very next morning. We'll wait, worried, scared, but knowing it is impossible to avoid this funeral at our familial home church! So. You have to come with me. It will help me be less terrified. Please. Hurry into the sanctuary in a rural town. And hide with me in that bright banner room.

Cry for a moment if you want to, or just stand there stunned by familiarity, seeing a child's landscape through an adult's eyes: all the white candle cupboards, red carpet, and hymnals lit with temperate morning light undeterred by the windows' old frosted glass. Don't kneel. Not yet! Stand hidden, stroking the emblazoned, embroidered fabrics that hang so quietly in their unseasonal disuse. Reach out! Go on; go ahead. Touch the textile sheep, lamé wedding rings, felt triplet crosses, percale Pentecost flames, satin white doves with ribbons in their beaks, metallic threads escaping the Star of Bethlehem over a manger's loosened stitching.

Don't worry about the funeral service. You've been to a hundred before. Oh. You haven't? Well. They're all the same. Someone says something. Not just something, always says the right thing, only not very well.

Good. Now. It's over. So. Come further. Come down those linoleum stairs that I ran up every Sunday in little patent leather shoes. Not the ones I wanted but the ones we could afford. Follow these few familiar men who carry Dad's casket down, down, down, so incrementally, so slowly, and shove it with exhausted reverence into the back of a hearse. Don't think about the suspension. The shocks are good enough. Just grieve with me. Hold a nearby hand when you just panic a little as a sound from twenty years ago returns. No? You didn't hear it? Let go, then, I guess, if you can't hear Daddy's intentional footsteps making their shined approach toward weekly grace.

47 — Man/Woman

It's okay to be a man. It's okay to be a woman. But what exactly happens if I tell you, "A friend of mine was raped on a balloon to the moon."?

When I tell you this, what else do you want to know to help form your opinion of the situation? Does it matter if my friend were a man or a woman? Does it matter if it were during the day or at night? Does it matter who was drunk or sober? What of risk-taking, beauty?

Does it matter if a child were conceived? What if my friend makes a decision?

Will there be a cordial reception?

The balloon to the moon is right on the safest way back to a home with pine siskins at the feeder.

28 — The End of Grief

For a few

motor-memory

years I sometimes got it and won,

found a forgotten child's game

in my gotta-get-me, left hand. But

now I no

longer hold my father's nose

(that sad, sorry, no-you-can't-have-it thumb-tip)

between two fingers,

absentmindedly.

29 — Cold Sunny Morning

A pleasant-looking woman dressed for a Saturday jog—
no work, no arrangement of hair—jerks the muzzled face of a
dog so it will perennially, assuredly, absolutely attend to her and
her Saturday morning perch on an abandoned bench chained to
the ice cream parlor.

30 — Inquiry

What constitutes a globe?

31 — Diary with Burning Ellipsis

But no, wait, the word is too charged. Let me put this in such a way that you don't just write the people off.

27 — Ladies Who Lunch on Disposable Plates

My mother and I arrived, recently, at an impasse. Chicago, disturbed as ever, hurried and swirled around us. We sat, stalemated, at an outdoor table after eating cheap Chinese food off paper plates with black plastic forks. It was hot, easily ninety degrees and humid.

If you have not ever been divorced you may not know its painful exposé of one's familial underbelly. High-reactive heartbreak originates in the present and stretches back into history—indiscriminately implicating relatives and selves along the way. Mothers resent it, which daughters resent. So there we sat.

Stilted and pissed off, we stood up and threw our paper plates away, moved out of the shady side of the street and crossed Adams to wait for the free tourist trolley.

Musing to herself without compassionate consideration of my situation my mother said that recently at a wedding a woman from Mom's office told the story of her own wedding.

In the telling, my mother gradually became more and more enraged. She explained how appalling it was that this woman—who had since had the nerve to get divorced—had the audacity to sit there and tell this story to my mother, in a church. It was savage. How dare she! And! Not only did this woman tell her own story of her own wedding to my mother but, unthinkably, she did it in front of her daughter, too.

My mother only believes in stable subjectivity.

So maybe it was the heat. Or her careless lack of compassion. Or the fact that if this woman had been married in the very same church where she was later attending a wedding, of course it would remind her of the day and she would mention it, no matter what happened subsequently. I said, "Why can't she tell the story of her wedding day just because she later got divorced?"

My mother said, "You're too hot."

32 — Laissez-Faire

I get up and rummage around on the coffee table digging through fifty unopened pieces of mail and discover a plastic bag from six months ago. In it? A well-designed box of Broncolin NF cough drops. Why? I don't know. It was an impulse purchase.

These are Hispanic cough drops and I am white.

I am not sick. But I never miss the sensational opportunity to linger over a cellophane-wrapped cardboard box, having long been a smoker.

I try not to drink Scotch in the morning. So, sitting down in the chair again, looking out over the water, I tease myself for a while, hesitating for a bit looking at the green human silhouette with the silver-rendered lungs and animated airway passages. These particular cough drops come "with echinacea and hedera helix." I finger the hologram and boldly weigh the net wt. 1.4 oz (40 g) of the *16 drops* contents on the palm of my open hand.

Then, with savagery, the cellophane comes off. I poke and prod at the box lid and rip the first sleeve of eight lozenges out of the package. With deft hands of experience I push against the bubble of plastic and push the dome down forcing the cough drop through the foil overlay.

Into my mouth it goes. The first cough drop. The only cough drop. There's a dizzying delight as the eucalyptus vapors enter my nasal passages. A rush of bliss. A torrent of salivation. A tongue numbed by pressure against the cough drop and the roof of my mouth.

Even my eyes burn, for a while.

43 — Conservative/Liberal

An impartial administration will preserve our deep democracy. Oh well. Here we go again. Out of storage, begin life, over and over and over. Prevent death, over and over and over. Sit transient but cedar attic-ed wearing a musty-vow wow-gown drinking some heat-slanting sun. I don't get it. Figure it out. Be a liberal/secular/democrat/scientific intellectual and a conservative/god-fearing/republican/evangelist. Hide the veil, silk-folded between pairs of underwear in a drawer you almost won't use for its lurking presence. Give up. Sell meaningless rings with their unending circular implications and do not think about disposable forms of forever. Dust-cover baby clothes and bassinets and other barren garages waiting to be consumed, later. Extract your favorite hymns from some indelible memory. Un-engrave dates and useless names. It's okay not to take sides, to let the napkins be insignificant, disposable even, to tell the difference between branching photos of ancestors whose stories end in your breathing in and out, in and out, hyperventilating for no reason— for any reason. Go on. Get up. Unbox porcelain swans, lift silver wings away from crystal and tarnished little spoons for generations of salt and needing dusting. Don't worry about MSNBCNNFOX boxes. Let tears dry over pity and fall in love with your own tightrope as if beached, cradled, and innocent. Let fingers reach through hairlines and find ears over and over and over. Let eyes enter rose beds mulched three inches thick with broken cocoa hulls. Come home between climate-controlled clotheslined sun-sheets holding onto horizontal summers where the people go. Taste frozen key limes on lip-skins as somehow enters each other's swallow-the-kiss. Love—God damn it— reenter me after the musty gown finds a consensual way to mildew as a Goodwill costume. How are you new-able to look at me that way? Just shut up for this one fucking minute. Just help me prevent death, over and over and over, help me begin life, over and over and over, out of storage.

33 — boy,

No reason, no rhyme. No way, navy boy. Better off naked with the aftersun blind squint. On leave Momma used to say, "I'm glad you were born girls so your father doesn't beatchu." So why did she dress me as a boy? Momma's momma always tattooed, "Wanted one, had one for a minute, 'fore he died," on the days on blue afternoons removed from 1940-what? Those holes in a wrong-made heart, that two-day blue baby, that boy. I ain't apologizing. Momma never did. Did she? Didn't have to. My daddy let me on his lap anyway—a *Let's read the Sunday funnies* girl, despite daddy's too-bad-about-it. Was that the grief at the dinner table? Too bad about the reasons. Too bad about the blues. Too bad about the boys born boys and beaten for it. Too bad about the girls born girls to mothers bereft of sons. Droves of women pulsing with resentment have nowhere to put shorn anchors pulled through an unforgiving decade of ribbed necks and navy blues. White caps, historic, heave into the crashing scream-sky. Boy. What boy? Baby blue grows up, grows wild, and collapses. Forget all that. Stay little. What can you carry on your cotton chest? Battleships, bugs, puffy school buses flaking apart, and paleontology, boy? Little girls play dress-up too: inadequate biceps flexing pretend proud in the deadweight lift of eyes.

65 — Ego Confronting Mortality

Dear Fake Advice Columnist,

My wife just had a kid. In terms of personal stability, I've recently taken a nosedive off the deep end. Thoughts?

Dear Ego Confronting Mortality,

I'm all for security, for turtle toys that cast weak-lit stars on the ceiling, and I definitely support your completely-and-totally-unprecedented-I-mean-seriously-never-before-experienced transition into fatherhood. You'll need a few traditions. Watch the role-playing. He doesn't deserve the backlash of resentment that's sure to follow if you abandon yourself. (And you don't deserve his reactionary rebellion that's sure to follow that.) Teach him about Shamrock Shake season. That'll shut him up.

34 — Lunch Alone

My Server's been a waiter at a little red-trimmed French restaurant as long as I've been going there. Today, he talked for an hour after I took his suggestion to order a glass of pinot blanc.

The squash soup and the *salade anchoiade* were on the table. With total control over my domain I placed the butter so that it would melt a bit in the sun. Three times My Server came to the table, offering his services. I said I was fine, repeatedly. However, he was not about to be put off. He finally came over to the table a fourth time and said, "I'm here, you know."

There are men with money and power. Others with great ideas, unfulfilled.

It seemed he needed to be needed. So, I put my pen and papers down, leaned back in the chair, and waited. Quickly, the story unfolded. He told me about his travels in Europe, his being a paramedic for a while, but how he didn't like letting people die when they had no proof of health insurance, how he considered getting on with the fire department, but that he didn't want to dumb himself down that much to fit in with the guys, how he'd been in real estate for a while, how he'd been in the restaurant business longer, how he liked to drink three glasses of white wine and wash it down with a beer, but that not enough places have a good wine list and a good beer list, and how he hated anyone thinking he was a pussy for wanting white wine; he explained that there was a great Neapolitan pizza place—coal fire and truffle oil— near Wellington & Ravenswood and a great new brewing company, Revolution Brewing Company, in the vicinity of Milwaukee & Fullerton, and also how he's getting married in June.

He had to excuse himself to answer the phone. I heard more as he spoke to someone else. He's Russian, a Russian Jew, with a Catholic grandmother, who took lots of antidepressants. The old woman at the bar was shocked that a Jew had ever married a Gentile. She tried to contain herself, but commended his family on their success, their triumph over social stigma. He said that his fiancée is not Jewish. This shocked the woman even more. "Don't you know the lineage goes through the mother?" Meaning, he should marry a nice Jewish girl. He said, "We just want to be happy."

My Server and the other server laughed at the man on the phone whose order was taken. Whoever it was became a detestable gargoyle in my mind: an individual incapable of trusting them to get his dinner right. I heard, "I'll give you two

French onion soups and a Nicoise salad. I know. No bread. Don't want you calling me back about sending you bread." He waited. Then said, "So, bread with the Nicoise salad?." Later, "I'll be looking forward to it."

The primary concern of the day was My Server's vision for the Cedar Hotel. He came back over and stood there daydreaming near the blue flowerpot with the red-and-yellow orchids pouting their polka dot lips, wearing his long white apron, white shirt, yellow-square-patterned red tie, and leaned forward on a leg up on the windowsill.

"Boutique hotel," he said, "like the Hotel Allegro downtown." We both stared at the eyesore across the street. I didn't know what to look for to see what potential he saw. But I waited, silent, and he showed me its value. Location is everything. The building was so close to Carmine's, to all the happenings on Rush. He had me. It was a great idea. I got excited, thought about spillover clientele, suggested a blues singer. He said, "No. Not that. No."

Sure. He knew the developer, a bit. Didn't think much of his choices to slap a neon sign on the front, stucco the ground floor, and open it up as a shit hole. My Server knew exactly what it would take. He knew what should be on the menu, how to get neighborhood signatures for a liquor license, how to decorate each of the rooms individually with great designers, how to get it up and running and make a great first impression.

I said, "How well do you know the owner?"

He said, "Not well enough to talk to him."

I said, "It sounds like you've got most of it figured out. You never know, he might be receptive. Get him on the right day. Get him in the right mood. He'll listen."

He didn't refute me, exactly.

We talked about structural integrity, gut rehab, what the rooms might look like on the inside, since it used to be a hotel for transients and the rooms have been shut up tight for at least five years. We talked about hotel developers, Miami's renovations, drug money in suitcases, and where to start.

36 — Get Rich & Save the U.S. Economy in the Process!

Sorting motivational accessories on Monday: bootstraps, grindstone, attitude, Calvin Coolidge's persistence for year two, Midwestern work ethic, humility, Che Guevara propaganda beret—size small—a whole pile of self hyphenates (e.g. self-reliance, self-control, self-determination, self-respect, self-sacrifice, etc.), then you get into the various abstract cultural ideals (freedom, liberty, 'Merican Dream, unity, solidarity). There's some leftover stuff, too. Like common purpose and shared vision. Not sure where those go.

You'll say, "I'm capitalizing!"

They'll be like, "Why?"

You're like, "I don't know. Isn't that what we're supposed to do? I want to own my own business, be my own boss, innovate, understand the new economy, and be part of what's happening now."

"Why?" "You can't." "You'll be one of them." "That's stupid." "It's too risky." "Aren't you a Democrat?" "No way.

That would never work out." "Do you even understand the tax implications?"

Pish-posh. It's fine that it seems nebulous. Give it credence. Give it time. What's to prevent us from having cockfighting rings in the basement on Tuesday nights?

But if you can stop the hurt from affecting anyone, from destroying anything, you win. Ten points. Keep your comments to yourself and just don't tip her so much.

"Yes! Let's do it."

70 — Virgin/Whore

Dear Fake Advice Columnist,

I got raped when I was in college. Most of my friends did too. I don't know why. It shouldn't be that big of a deal. I don't even really remember it. Disembodied trauma and shit. But I was wondering if I could have a normal sex life again. Nothing elaborate, just a sweet loving connection with the man I love.

Dear Virgin/Whore,

No. What are you talking about? You shouldn't even think about having any kind of sweet loving connection. Who the hell do you think you are? Plus. That's all a bunch of brainwashing, propagandistic bullshit. You're liberated! Don't let yourself get hamstrung by Laura Ingalls Wilder. It's all crap, another created market branded to sell you off into a cult of prim piety. So. No. This is what you tell that sentimental sap of a boyfriend of yours: *Why would I consult you? I got lessons from a real live dominatrix who showed me a contraption for home use on her sales floor. What? Nothing you say now matters anyway. I already spent the money. Just shut up and listen while I parrot her sales pitch about how this key-to-vinyl-heaven comes in a variety of custom colors. You like red. You should be happy. You wanted a surprise for your birthday. Just get over here, hand me the Allen wrench, and deal with it. This thing converts into seven pieces of furniture. I don't remember what all the contortions are called. Only "fuck bench" lingers in my mind.*

12 — Ma Deuce

That summer night, before I joined the army, I thought swimming would mean we'd hop a fence in some Canadian neighborhood. But no. We drove out onto a back road and then further down a rutted grass path covered with trees until the guy's car gave up and stopped.

I was drunk enough. As soon as I got out of that car I heard the roar, saw low orange clouds. Two guys, boys really, took us down a path to some sort of trestle or crane that reached out over the Niagara River. Now I don't know the exact distance we were upstream from the falls. But I know the river was already anxious about going over that edge. Swift currents rushed over rocks. Eddying shifting waters surged in smooth swells nearby. Right under the trestle the water was just one smooth silk curl and deep enough. If I had to guess conservatively, I'd say we were less than a mile upstream from the falls. I shudder to think how close we really were.

Civilization now has nothing to do with simpering sets of crossed ankles and ungloved fingers reaching for tea cakes. A woman has only to do with regulations. It's a life of don'ts. One can only stand so long at a kitchen sink, pouring simple glasses of homemade lemonade. Such god damned relegation. A woman is not to enjoy standing under some inundating Niagara, or to love the concussion of the falls, to feel the doom-damning imminent thrill of maybe, just maybe, accidentally going over the falls.

No one should, I guess. It's not about equal rights anymore. It's really more a safety concern. Still I think, "But what of Liberty?"

A more secure woman wouldn't have joined the army, but I did and stood in a tiny little shed above the night-fire course in the Ozarks. I was with a drill sergeant who manned a machine gun. He shot live rounds out over the soldiers from my platoon, friends, who were low-crawling under barbed wire getting tear gas powder in their mouths. I backed into the corner of the shed and watched the shell casings pile up on the floor. He said to me, "Jones. You're one of those serious privates, aren't you?"

I had a huge crush on this guy. He was hot, skinny, rugged, and drove a cherry red classic convertible Mustang from the '60s. But when he said to me, "Jones. You're one of those serious privates, aren't you?" while magnesium flares burst over the live-fire training field where two hundred of my friends were, that crush ended.

I agreed, I suppose. Who knows?

Not then but later, I thought back to the night I jumped into the Niagara River so close to those falls. Before deciding to go for a swim with the guys we met, this friend and I went out after her mom had gone back to the hotel. We met the guys at the bar. They followed us onto the street. Then we all four wandered. You know, somewhere together with nowhere in mind. I don't remember climbing onto the roof of a grocery store. But we did and tossed rocks near the feet of unsuspecting pedestrians. You'd toss a stone and then watch a woman look all around for the culprit. Invariably, she'd never look up. Women don't. We did not throw rocks at men.

Anyway, after we grew tired of this grocery store roof game, one of the guys must have said, "You girls want to go swimming?"

So what if I was a serious private a few months later?

Who knows who jumped from the trestle first, but when it was my turn I fell somewhere between ten and thirty feet to the water. That stupendous current accepted my body like nothing ever had. I swam like crazy for the bank. I think my friend may have jumped more than once, but I'm pretty sure that once was enough for me. I knew I'd reached some kind of limit of my daring. I don't think I was the only one. After a couple of jumps each we found what privacy was available as couples and made out on the high cement pylons.

The drill sergeant ended up disgusted with me in that machine gun shed a few months later and seemed to feel I'd ruined his evening with my thoughtful awareness. Canadian boys on cement pylons are one thing. But it might have been nice to end up making out with this hot drill sergeant in the little shed with that .50 caliber machine gun. Instead he was all pissed off about me being so serious, so aware of bullets ripping out pieces of the sky. I didn't apologize. What had I done but stare grieving into the night?

I accidentally stepped backwards onto his hat when my feet were almost covered in shell casings. That did it. He could never forgive me now.

At the river above the falls, I can't remember the structure we were on, not really. I've tried to revisit the place in my mind, but there are only puzzle pieces that don't fit well with lemonade glasses in hospitable hostess hands or with feet burning in sun-penetrating spit-shined Airborne boots. But I remember falling from a rusted, jagged, abandoned metal transom jutting out over the water from two huge cement pylons. I remember going down, down, deep down, under an orange sky cloud-filled.

Those obfuscating cumulus vapors lay lowered right on top of

the sodium lights and roar.

38 — Grotto

Her: Can you really contrive: a simple morning where the faded curtains lift out and away from a lovely dirty weathered-wood sill? For almost a million dollars you can buy a painting of a scythe in storage.

Him: It's up to me to learn, to teach, to know, to shatter the mug thrown and unharness its breakage, to witness its fall, then, again to harbor her remnants.

Her: I wake up under a dumpster. I'm bound and gagged in a makeshift body bag. My neck nearly strangled with duct tape. I hear a slow bent vehicle in reverse, beeping, blue, warning pedestrians.

Him: Do not love me symmetrically. Get out of here and let me shave.

Her: If not that man, who is with me in the lightening and darkening of the sky with these stations of the cross, these mulched honorariums where iris and geraniums share the quiet with koi swimming near eternal and not so eternal flames flickering—purchased in earnest, in contemplative red desperation?

Him: Thank God we don't have to stand looking through a hundred yards of pine trunks, across manicured evening grass, to the infant fields of rising corn—momentarily allowing for the fireflies—together.

Her: Exchange the lovemaking for life, for coming undone from the duct tape inside, for produce and bounty, for the bus pass, parking space, and retirement fund. Walk away. If you can, wait for the bus, alone. Do not call anyone in the sunshine under blue skies and don't kick the children just because they're not yours.

Him: I don't see anything happening, like water moved by tail fins.

42 — Centripetal/Tangential

She flips the channel. There must be a way to replace the
mind. Stand up for peonies, pink. The stems are cut and crystal
bubbles and rush filling goes under the faucet. Brunette fosters
herself, again. Vases of flowers cold and wet should be carried
with two hands and placed carefully down on a shifted white
bookcase with a blue lake view. Hot air comes to look through
the crystal, water, and stems. The air leaves embarrassed evidence
of its hot-on-cold. Drops. Someone brunette should sit down,
damn it, and wonder how cold vases surrounded by humidity can
begin to draw rivers, oceans, and lakes out of the sky.

44 — Creative/Destructive

Men move without ever turning their heads to see if, maybe, someone they know is right behind them. Whereas women just run. They know. They know for sure. She is backed into a corner with a doe. Their four eyes rattle and scan the darkened rooftops. She wears a pinafore and wields a blazing torch; it is no use.

Nothing of disproportion remains even if you cut the fingers off elastic lace gloves to let red talons cross the wrenched sky with cigarettes, even if you ignore the tattooed sign of a thresher for sale. In God we trust. And there are no pink flamingos staked into the lawns on the money. What do we do to stop denying our destructive pram-sugar-cube culpability? "We don't need another loan," to acknowledge that greatest creator and greatest destroyer in a world of dreamscapes all filmed against a Southern California backdrop. Instead of looking up with blame and asking, "Why, God?" hold up a squealing piglet as if Lady Liberty gripped it by the hind feet. Let the crowd of extras get paid to clap to the beat whether they're wearing bandanas, beards, fishnets, dress boots, or purple suits.

A planned demolition exists between a woman in chains and a man in a red muscle shirt. She's got her suitcase all ready to go. He's screaming in long johns. Grand. That is their legacy. Or maybe stately is the best description for that broken row of lakeside weeping willows ruined by a storm's wretched winds.

For years they lined up and spilled down from some humidity-laden sky. During a storm intermittent ones were struck, killed, then chipped, chain-sawed and hauled off. Wind, unknown here, is more real than anything made with dry ice and a fog machine. We fight hardest for all that we are entitled to but must be aware that we are fighting not only for the best that we deserve but also, with the subversive nature of self-destruction, the worst.

Who cares about the bolo tie, the red dye job, and the high school smiles? As Americans we must stop the entitled acquisition of our deservings.

Fuck. We may have to bow down, humbly, and acknowledge, "Oh God." Even with a hookah on a mushroom it seems, "We need a good price." It's the same in the quarry, in the brick barn, in the parking lot, with the mulch man, or cheered up with a big brother's bright birthday bouquet of Mylar balloons.

Just do it. Just say good-bye.

The woman with the suitcase drives between the wilted lake and the blinking lined-up high-rises, soothed by her someday after an electric sky, entranced by the coming and going water meter owners on the bicycle path and also by this oncoming trafficked Lake Shore Drive—and oh God, the ache fall. Because we will damn well get it. Oh God, the lightning crack in half and wood from which life barely knows the swirling flood in a sewer gutter splayed everywhere, and weight-bearing bent drowning branches in the grass.

45 — Identity/Id entity

Under bedrock, the world moves molten. It seems not at all possible when confronted by that crust of seeming solidity. But denial is dangerous. You and I both know that rock subverts great flows of magma. And below your exterior, your countenance, your pleasant tolerance, the self melts where mountains have yet to be made. You want a steam vent? I've got just the nothing causing that kind of defeated hunt for entrance. We both know there's a way in. Because we see every kind of shattered earth: snowy streetlight near cracked asphalt in a parking lot, but also bedrock asunder, and exploding meadows. This is your version of loving, eh? Okay. But I have diligently done all that, picking over soft filth, pretending. Another damned mess made just to be cleaned up. Shhhh! I know. We don't have to talk about it. It will go away. I'll sift glitter and dust across that place where a steam vent can't exist because I must obstruct my loving, knowing entrance to you. Just hush. Let the glitter come down through nothing, falling dutifully bright, and likewise weightless, flat. Don't say anything. Not another word. Let this silence of my shaken may-as-well-go-on morning be like powdered sugar on a Bundt cake. Uniform, perfect ash drifts down just the way nothing's swept away from the dusted dark, which remains as its own reality. We may be able to prove and disprove ourselves sinister and sane continually. Just shut up about it. Get some slivered almonds on the way home, will you? And to these beginnings be, blessed white fires of belonging, undone and rapt, and so Pinatubo, so what? Rim unclosed and somehow surging, so much molten earth forced into our night sky—how can it be? It is. Not a cake. Not a steam vent. Not any kind of horrid, unprecedented eruption. Not anymore. It is nothing in the morning. Only. Undone and cooling wrapped valley spurs, through obsidian eyes, and so leave these unquestioned, these blessed white fires of belonging: me, yours, your only own pyroclastic flow.

60 — Pussy/Deterrent Threat

Dear Fake Advice Columnist,

I'm a guy and I'm sort of a pussy. Sometimes I sit around with all my friends and talk about what a bunch of pussies we are. Check this shit out. A girlfriend of one of my buddies was on a train. Right in front of her this old man was severely beaten and mugged. It was crazy. She had to sit there and witness it. Just watch someone get brutalized and robbed. She was really shaken. We tried to make her feel better, help her relax. Just kept talking about how much we would have showed that guy a thing or two. But you know what? Honestly? I'm glad I wasn't there. I probably would have had to do something.

Dear Pussy/Deterrent Threat,

It might not have happened if you were there.

49 — Security/Insecurity

I had a dominant dependence on several men in a row. What? No. That can't be right. (Nobody looks good in a thong.) Wait, watch, wild, wonder, world over, skill, better, improve, perform, control, get, do. This is my insecurity: that it is me, that it is not. For forty-two minutes and twenty-eight seconds a man in jeans with his shirt off gets a mechanical lap dance. So hurried; then a woman lies down on a sandy path between green aloe bushes. She's secluded, ready, wanting. But never secure. There's nothing to tie her to: no mooring, no cleat, no tree, no bike rack, no fence post, no tow bar. What will hold her weight if a storm comes? She is free in the confidence-shifting sands and wears that brick red nothing. Get mesmerized. Go to Milan with a fresh manicure and pedicure. Do it May 30, 2011; October 8, 2011; February 12, 2011; October 7, 2011; September 6, 2011; March 27, 2011; May 24, 2011; July 17, 2011. Indecision grows more powerful in its acquisition, rationalizing any means necessary as a mode of conquering and ascension. No matter what there is a metallic plastic superhero with disproportionate tits French inhaling in a midnight blue solitude. The ember tip of her cigarette lights the contours of her hand, her cheek, her nose, her breast, her shoulders. She's been working on her deltoids, her biceps, her triceps, her lats. Devastation ensues. (Address victim/victor, predator/prey, dominance/submission, acceptance/rejection, and the rest of interpretive inflexibility here.) The metallic plastic superhero hunches forward exhausted by exertion against defeat.

Her back curves slightly, shoulders forward. No one would dare ask: *What is she thinking?* We'll never know. The bootleg copy of her adventure is spliced. Her thoughts get lost in translation. Remember those animated teach-kid-a-ma-things, Mr. Men and Little Miss? Like Kool-Aid people. Remember? Well, there they are. Three of them. Blown way out of proportion, climbing over buildings like Godzilla. They stalk through their minimalist city finally ending up between a riverfront and the bay. Blue. Red. Yellow. Primary and smiling.

Let them fill the sky. Is it an objective goal to have to build something permanent when one is so simply impermanent? Creative destruction is our, "This is how it is. It's natural. It's okay." They can say it with emotional appeal or just statistics, whichever you prefer.

I get it that we have varied ideas about security and freedom, that we all feel our beliefs should have a revelation. Good. Let them fill the sky. This time it's a flesh-burst sunset sky, not that cloud cover where the animated shoulds conquer everything. I'm talking about a beach with thirty feet of wet hardpack sands that reflect twilight. I get it. A man, muscular as a matter of course, does footwork there with a soccer ball. He is out of the way of crashing surf. But here's how it is: he is barefoot. There's no reef, not here. Fingerling distant man-made things reach out from the beach, from the shore, into the destructive breakers to say, "Hey. Slow down, why don't cha?"

Silhouettes of five naked women pose in the high grasses. Targets and arrows help direct sunlight and perspective. The purple flowers of wild onions never bend even though these five naked silhouettes are captured dancing: hands on cocked hips, spinning hair, carelessly-tossed arms, a tight ass, a high-heeled foot kicked up, boobs bending forward, chest out, back arched, head up, feet crossed at the ankles, and the last woman bent over grabbing her ankles to prove the point, to make sure it was absolutely clear: there is no limit to the resources we'll put behind our conviction.

Repeat after me: Every man is a mother's son. There's a basset hound in the backseat. Every life is precious. A woman rests against her man. She's spent, wet, pleasured. Watch her trace the contours of her abs with the stem of a red flower. But when it comes down to it, justice can prevail. And did.

As topics of conversation go WWII was black-and-white. Like porn and highway budgets. You cannot put people in ovens and call that a country. Satin constricts the cleavage that spills out from under a borrowed fedora. That is unacceptable or fine. But Vietnam, Afghanistan, Iraq? I don't know. There's a real discussion there.

Look. Fuck deliberation and diplomacy. I'm not involved in all that. I'm just talking about something to say over dinner with a couple bottles of wine. Maybe you can beat up on the Kurds, you know, just a little. One pole dancer with fishnet sleeves plays chess with another in a tiger-striped string bikini. Maybe you can bully each other with sectarian strife. What's a lost life here and there? Here's a sudsy pillow fight to distract you.

Who needs a conservative backlash? Those girls—all of them, the five naked silhouettes, the pole dancer in the fishnet sleeves, the other one in the tiger-striped string bikini—curl up together, satisfied, asleep. I think we play a lot. All of us have amazingly playful lives. (Of COURSE paintball is awesome, hello! And this is the most awesome ruse squad EVER!! Helicopters?!

Um, sign me up. We would TOTALLY kick ass. Anytime. I will go, anytime.)

For blond curls and bending back over fence rails. She doesn't have to take off her jelly bracelets. Cubs roll around, squabbling in a meadow so they'll be able to grow up and tear each other to shreds for food, mates, and territory. Focus on the screen: let her come toward you, come down from that height, come toward you, let her come toward you, let her come, let her come toward you, smiling, let her come down, let her come toward you, let her come off the lava rocks and jump down into the sand, let her come toward you.

So the question is, in our indulgence, in our play, for what are we preparing? What skills and powers are we refining? In what areas are we becoming great?... Read More

Or don't. There's a huge agave plant. We are trained and prepared. Crow wings reflect morning sunlight. But for what? What will the actions of our lives be? Let her come toward you in the sunlight of a soccer ball-bouncing beach. Let her smile, jump, plunge, dive, and surface, crushed. Why? I guess for the party by the pool.

Get pushed in by the thousands. He's not the only one. None of us is. You're not. She's not. I'm not. Everyone values money for the freedom it represents. Release balloons. Make out.

Carry your camera—always carry your camera—wag your ass, bungee jump between the sound stages, kneel down with another shaved girl. There are many other values that we project onto the concept of *financial independence*. (Isn't that whole idea passé?) No one has to actually say it in a yellow follow spot that crosses the crowd and makes patterns with the red one: beat, beat, beat, lines of light up and down, back and forth, crossing, uncrossing, lighting faces, bodies, clothes, hats, skin, and abandoning all of it as quickly.

No one cares. It's normal. It's fun. It's what you do.

But, this Fake Paintball War might just be the most amazing display of freedom…ever!

That girl with the great hair wears a watercolored ruffle that obscures and accentuates her tits. I can appreciate that because I have a great respect for my friends who prioritize freedom over security.

The applications of the balance of Freedom and Security are everywhere. There's a baby in headphones helping the DJ. It is everything from War to cell phone record Big Brother Surveillance stuff to getting your neighbor to stop letting his dog shit in your yard.

There's no pit of vipers under the hood. If you know where you are on the spectrum, then you can start to understand where others are on that same spectrum.

Maybe you aren't the guy who wears a rainbow thong to commemorate Stonewall. Maybe that guy prioritizes Freedom just a little bit more than you. Or maybe you aren't the person who could detonate a Claymore mine to protect your rights. Maybe that guy prioritizes Security just a little bit more than you. Or vice versa. How should I know?

Well, thank God for you both, I say. Because if the Claymore guy is blowing up other people so we can sit around and live in fearful closets, that's no kind of fun. And, if the guy in the rainbow thong doesn't have a trigger-happy bodyguard, well, let's face it, somebody's definitely going to fuck his shit up.

As an individual and as a nation—what does "what we want" look like? Put on the floppy, pink fur hat as we extrapolate this conceptualization to the enactment of our lives in Isla Mamey. There are ways that we want to exert ourselves in the world. One way is to drape a string of beads, loose, over your belly and let it drape-cross your back.

17 — Carefully Placed Patterned Pavers

They were the only two people on an officially-dedicated pedestrian bridge—its plaque still new, telling who the mayor was, who the deciders were, ready to age well in the elements, riveted indestructible bronze to the concrete bridge.

Who were they? Strangers. A girl and a grifter. There were no handcrafted cocktails. She was doing homework outside. An article sat flapping in her lap. The homeless man just stopped wandering nowhere and asked her, "Are you reading?"

She looked up at the beard and brown arms, the paper bag and smile. Wind spiked bright with September; what encounter is there, really? She offered a response. Not an answer really, though.

The green shirt walked on toward sultans and saints, toward re-invented elastic driveway gate Toledo girls rinsed sulfate-free. Toward a castoff mid-weight cotton blend twill reversible two-tone jacket.

Wabash River water oozed beneath their distancing departure. He had been right to ask. Who could read with so many beautiful distractions—the cicadas, flagpoles, shadows, and breeze?

She noticed how suddenly he was gone, with the water, and the wind, and the road of hum-cars, which had long since streamed on by.

50 — Smart/Dumb

Tip back, pop, inhale acetone until fluttering wings are stilled to rigor. Romantic people—men and women—forced to pretend to be dumber get no happy, furry, Benji chrysalis base camp. Only anesthesia.

If, when walking home, a reflection accosts you, offer it something sweet. Sunglasses. Posture. A little rouge. Because that shimmering reflecting pool will shore you up and follow you home, riding shadows that at least exist under your sole, if nowhere else. They are waiting to grow more, if only conditions get sunny and slant.

Fumes suppress neither the will nor the inevitability of a transformation. He looks. Look away. Commute polite within the smell of a creosote hoard's careful descent with perpetual monotony of never-meetings. Hush, girl. Flip-flop. Flip-flop. Betray quiet general blessings. Soap up silent curses of an entire demographic segment of your own neighborhood's residential population. Stay with them and come down temporary railway construction stairs together. They are a sector of society swarming home from work. There is no each other suffering an internal combustion in one of those hopefully deniable hearts. Do not think: *And still my life is a slow revolution on melting kite-type days.*

How? Monies get paid for lemonade frozen slush, small grains of sand falling out of suits; assess this as some *good enough.* Fine. Don't fight it, the setting of the mold, a demur, resignation of disposable ego. (The facades and fronts and lies go here.) Reality screams itself undone, "Real it, why?" Be cause. And knowing that, don't ever ask forgiveness.

So then turn slightly with the whirled, turn toward another shiny surface and smile. Keep your chin down for the photo. Get more highlights. Give up your mind. It has no cultural currency—certainly not any bearing on the mating game—where bullfighters reign supreme. Power through the takedown. Naps, etcetera, and rain. Days later find the moment past exactly where pink blown-foam ridges came down railway construction stairs— hot flip-flopping, pulling up an unfelt tarry print, this impression of the melt, the material structure, adhesive, and the poor recanted light.

51 — Subjective/Objective

An eye found heaven in humidity's weight pressed, foiled, startled even, by an almost forward motion. Dissection? Of what? Sailing tea pots sink halfway down into illustrated oceanic pages with soldiers and animated dump trucks, happy, broad-smiled, big-eyed and American. (Right to work! Right to life!) But you have not replied. Sauna surfers cut through mock waves of a comic book culture bored of asserting: I am not a communist or an intellectual. Books don't just write themselves. Here is evisceration, and here is black wax. This sheer will arises out of recanting and weakness. No rebuttal? Fine. Look here, though! No, Look! What about these: plastic, permissive, permutation, permeable, perhaps, all pliable, all the acceptable ply would except you. So there must be another objective reason that can liberate us from all this yammering subjectivity. Don't talk to me about any individual's perceived illusion. Who would assert some thermodynamic principle about what fluid kinetic model bears meaning? Silly. Arrangement creates meaning. What else would? Someone has to be to blame. Of course there's an author. So.

Shut up. Don't talk to me about alternatives. Gimme another dissecting tray. Bring enough pins to hold back the skin. The objective point of view has nothing to do with two generations of Martin on the beach with a Mobius strip, a twist in a strip of paper held out in a young man's hand to a child unsure. Perceive this: the real thing and the impossible concept fused—resolved by being undeniable. Don't forfeit your witness of a stillicide. Don't stand up just to unbutton a dress. Don't give momentary dollars and leashes to red-haired mange beard beggars. Don't forget birthdays and specificity or graves. Don't maul or maraud or madden or crowd. Don't you dare. But damn. Oh, hello, Virginia's Septemberish brambling-ocean-masted day. How did you manage to camouflage these ships, barques, and liners?

7 — Commuted Fantasy

Some woman thought: *That man really isn't anything to look at on his riding mower. Not good-looking. But. Don't tempt me while I drive past this hillside lawn being mown on a diagonal. I'm liable to grab the edger and pitch in. It'd be downright adulterous.*

52 — Tangible/Intangible

I have fallen down into my pulse. Twice. Aunt Ginerva never knew. She stood unbuttoning her blouse on the other side of the wall I painted battleship gray. Still I heard her sigh through the panels from the other side of the family. Even though the paint was wet, I leaned my forehead against the wall. Burdened, I sat down, turning, on the low wooden stepladder, felt the wet smear drying, forced myself to rub the paint away. In front of me the bramble filled with motion: sparrows and wind. I stepped forward, pruned my way into all the consumer culture shit of greenery with paint-splattered tennis shoes filling up sandy-soled. This is. It didn't seem like it. Not enough like the blue moons over Meigs Field where those wide pupils in black-eyed Susans stood shedding their hot-wilt petals near the green goldenrod readying itself between seasoned runways overcome under displaced skylines attuned to how all the self-actualization of objective correlatives fuel futility class strife in the name of upward mobility. What to do? Dunno. Bare skin. Eyes have looked me over but not like yours, love. Please. Don't. Wait.

Dammit, sometimes on Easter Sunday in a little town where skies pressed down against the river-eroding backyard and gave up against ground-up loam, my father wore a burgundy beret and taught me how to drive a stick. Where are you going? Come back. Listen. My father wore that same burgundy beret in a little town that wait-watched the corn and ostentatious soybeans. Even so things of value have shifted back to the intangible. Haven't they? It is hard to hold anything memorable but your hand, Dead Daddy. Here in some store you never knew about, I'm holding a hexagonal jar of Tupelo honey. If I hold it hard enough the glass might cave in, waxen, or it might shatter, and honey-stick drip-slow to thick shards and drop bloody honey down.

94 — Stalker

Dear Fake Advice Columnist,

I live in Chattanooga, Tennessee. I was thinking about coming to see you so I could track you down, look in your windows, and maybe freak you out when you're on your way to the mailbox or something.

Dear Stalker,

That is amazing! I was just thinking that I could really use a semi-nefarious form of validation. I live in Chicago. I'm not sure if you'll fly or drive. But I figure if you really want to intimidate me with your voyeurism, you'll have a car for all the surveillance equipment. The drive is beautiful this time of year. It's almost a straight shot. Just go towards Nashville and then take I-65 North until it almost ends at the toll road (that's 90.) Drive west towards Chicago. It'll cost you about 5 dollars but saves a hellish hour of unnerving traffic. Take the Stony Island exit north to Lake Shore Drive. Trace the eastern perimeter of Chicago as far as Belmont. Park your car wherever you end up. Don't drive further than two blocks in any direction after you exit. Put your hazards on. Set up your tripod. You'll find plenty of places to mount your 64-bit compatible, remote internet monitoring, weather resistant (IP66), 40-foot night vision, IR cut filter (day/night), remote connect H.264 compression-capable cameras. You're always welcome!

56 — Glory-Seeking Adulator

Dear Fake Advice Columnist,

Why should anyone listen to you?

Dear Glory-seeking Adulator,

What memories you inspire! Once at night, during a passionate summer romance when my lover held his wet, naked body against my own in an earthen furrow among endless rows of grapevines on an Italian hillside, he asked me the same question.

58 — Hatemonger

Dear Fake Advice Columnist,

Sometimes I hate everything for no reason.

Dear Hatemonger,

Fear more the undoing night. Allow your mind to succumb to foot-stamping must-have-to-shoulds. Demand your every-which-way and now. Do not think about rocks in a river. Rage at them even if they're just meditative. Do not begin to accept that if you were traveling downstream by boat, the rocks would be a constant threat to your vessel. But please—please— don't dare consider the other view that if instead you were crossing that river on foot, there might be a way to use those exact same rocks to help traverse what could drown you.

15 — The Dumbass Solidarity Project: A Facebook Forum

Currently, the public school media political church system in America breeds a bunch of dumbasses who have virtually no ability to assimilate facts into opinion. Our critical thinking and reasoning skills have become dulled by self-indulgent modes of subjective punditry. It is my belief that anxiety can be diminished not so much by constant gratification alone but also the more an individual understands available facts in a context of informed opinion.

The dichotomies in our cultural conversation make it difficult for us to communicate as Americans. Leaders prey upon our collective inability to process information.

This forum is going to be a place where experts and dumbasses can intermingle safely in a respectful online forum so we can further the American conversations related to matters of public policy, religion, philosophy, finance, and ethics. Developing skills related to discussion, debate, and articulate delivery of information can help an individual gain a comfort level with his or her opinions and their assertion. We need to ask and answer questions of each other. We need to speak to those with whom we'd never interact.

It really means a lot that I'm not the only dumbass with an interest in the best use of logical fallacy, a malaise of generalized dismissal, and the condescending tone of sardonically saturated sarcasm for the purposes of winning at all costs in pretty much any earthly form of one-on-one rhetorical debate.

If you don't know whether you are a dumbass or an expert, don't worry about it. Everyone is welcome.

A FOLLOW-UP STATEMENT ISSUED TO THE DUMBASS SOLIDARITY PROJECT — REGARDING ITS IMMINENT DEMISE:

I just want to take a moment to say how vapid and meaningless the past few months have been for me.

90 — Cycle of Victimization

Dear Fake Advice Columnist,

I get victimized a lot. It's okay, not that I like it, but I'm used to it. I grew up with it, married into it, divorced myself and got more of it, and can't imagine any other way of approaching my life. It works really well. Right when I start to think maybe there's a problem with the situation and muster the nerve to discuss it, the man I am with just tells me I'm crazy. I know he's right.

So those liberated years went by: Rape. Domestic intimidation. Abuse. Control. Manipulation. Guilt. Shame. Screaming. No help except some pills. They're supposed to fix what's so obviously wrong with me. He doesn't take pills. There's nothing wrong with him.

I don't call the cops. My husband and my mother wouldn't approve. But I'm sitting here on the floor in the kitchen, my forehead bleeding from where he beat me with the cordless.

I don't really have a question because I don't actually want to ask. I don't have the courage anyway. But, I guess I'm just wondering if I should go to the hospital, or do you think maybe it's better if I just take care of this head wound myself? I may even have some gauze and medical tape in the upstairs bathroom.

Dear Cycle of Victimization,

I wish I were a man so I could give you some better, more authoritative advice.

Still, good for you for not involving the authorities. Your socioeconomic status really doesn't allow it. No one would understand. Cops are for poor people. Patrol cars shouldn't come to your kind of neighborhood.

You don't need my help or the cops' help anyway. You know the drill. Totally cut yourself off from all honest human contact in an effort to save face. Do whatever you have to do to keep up that good front. Do something meaningless, disconnected, alienated, alone. Decorate baskets. Isolate if you can. Deny abject humiliation. Stop breathing so much all the time.

And, really, whatever the form, no matter how private you think this connection is, it's safer for you to put this text away. Your current husband's going to be so pissed off if he sees you reading the paper, or the book, or the e-reader, or the smart phone, or the computer screen, or the PDF print-out, or the HTML 5, the unsupported EPUB 3 or wherever it is that we can find a way to interact. Come on. Aren't you scared? Even I'm terrorized. So don't drag me all into the situation. I don't want to be involved in this with you. The minute he walks in, he's gonna know it's about him.

59 — Detritus

Dear Fake Advice Columnist,

I love taking responsible action. The problem is I don't really do anything and don't really care. If you get this letter, someone took the wadded-up paper with one stupid hopeful sentence on it and mailed it to you for no good reason.

I can't imagine any of my friends getting anything out of my trash unless I'm getting some kind of recycling lecture. So probably my question to you will just molder away in a landfill, expedited by a layer of decaying guacamole.

Yeah. That's what'll happen. My friends don't take much initiative in real life. That's where I live: real life. It's got different rules than where you live. Actually, now that I think about it, I don't even know if you're going to be able to give me any helpful advice, because I mean, real people operate pretty differently than you do. They almost never do stuff like rescue important thoughts on paper. Either they aren't around, or they don't realize someone even had a personal moment of inspiration and then—embarrassed—threw away the evidence.

61 — Infantile

Dear Fake Advice Columnist,

Sometimes I hate authority. Especially that venture type with otherworldly hourglass figures and unbounded futures chalice aloft. I just cannot abide how they come right in wearing mirror sunglasses over unfulfilled hopes. Yes, sometimes I really want someone to just tell me what to do. But then when someone does, I always hate it. How can I resolve my overly-entitled American sense of infantilism?

Dear Infantile,

Never fear and listen up: I'm going to tell you what to do! I am in charge! And I'm really not willing to listen to anything you have to say, unless I get to thwart you and punish you and control you and become a dominant overbearing force in your life. I will shoot you down for no good reason and—if you know what's good for you—you'll thank me for it. Alternatively, like in the case that you make a point? I'll dismiss you from my life summarily. All this talk of equality only goes so far. You're of no use to me unless I can rely upon your servitude. So there is no reason to resolve anything between us diplomatically. Dependence is requisite if we're to remain in contact.

35 — Breast Meat

Breast meat at about 138 degrees pulled from the bird and then mango chutney. Salt necessarily. And ice water—after the ice has melted completely. If I must be pursued, then with that kind of predatory playing-house romance eat steamed sweet carrots or pearl onions and garlic roasted with celebrity status. And if even further supplementation (wellness comes from vitamins) is necessary, fine, then I suppose sweet potato pie topped with pecans. All knees bent for writhing unconscious. If you are still not satisfied, and Lord, it seems you never are, then get up, go to the fridge, get the fries out, and eat them in their cold ketchup Styrofoam hangover corner. And then in the morning, if you happened to stay, bring the paring knife and the fruit rot back to the bed. Talk some on a flat-backed morning and pull the knife through; cut me off some sustaining pear petals. The skin chew-slips. And the fruit chew-slips. And you know that moment when four feet resist the floor? Linger there. Un-till fields, these horizons of childhood, these memories of the plains.

62 — Patriotic Anomaly

Dear Fake Advice Columnist,

I could not give a fuck about my country.

Dear Patriotic Anomaly,

But I think my worst offense was just being part of it all. I remember all this gungho bullshit. What I've done is learn how to balance myself on the tightrope. All this rah-rah sensationalism and hyperbole that was supposed to convince me and rile me up and scare me and make me stop thinking for myself.

And I remember thinking, "This is ridiculous." Because there I was in a foxhole in the rain. Not a real foxhole in a real war. But a pretend foxhole in a controlled environment. My glasses were fogged up. My Kevlar helmet kept tipping forward, which pushed my glasses down, and that pulled my hair since there was an elastic strap that kept my glasses on my face. I stood on two cinder blocks, trying to balance one on the other end to end, so that I would be tall enough to maintain my position in the foxhole (which was really a section of sewer conduit on its end driven six feet into the ground with gravel in the bottom), and my position consisted of balancing my chin on a plastic gun made by Mattel, leaning my hands on sandbags turned to concrete in the rain then sun then rain then cold solidification of what can no longer be molded, not falling asleep in the rain behind foggy lenses, and most importantly on exuding the general impression of seeming to give a shit.

63 — Wannabe

Dear Fake Advice Columnist,

Sometimes I pretend I'm stupid, because it's cooler.

Dear Wannabe,

You're stupid.

54 — Hammered

Dear Fake Advice Columnist,

Sometimes I get hammered and pick fights with people who are hammered too.

Dear Hammered,

In general, it's a good idea not to antagonize drunken strangers. (Especially not that guy.) Displacement can be misconstrued. When you find yourself commiserating with a mutually-petty drunken friend about the inability of the waitress to provide a replenished bowl of salty stale popcorn just within earshot of the thuggish bruiser who has long had a crush on the poor girl and won't let her get past him without his insisting upon her opinion about his latest TROUTMASTER blog entry, try not to say something off-topic like, "Hey, Dickweed, move your fat ass."

64 — Meaningless Existence

Dear Fake Advice Columnist,

I'm one of them. I mean, I'm deathly afraid my friends won't like me in a still shot of a place I don't recognize. I'm in silver and plaid, sweating through harmonica music notes in a stadium crowded with wild abandon and 50,000 assigned seats. I'm a rebel. But I never do anything really too wrong. I would never wear paisley or jockey silks. I wouldn't play any instrument with a reed after eighth grade. Maybe drums. Maybe the bass. I'm afraid of messing up my future, implicating my family, and drawing the friendly fire of morally relativist judgment. I don't want the microphone. I don't want to dust off home plate. I won't wear a beret or eat oranges in public. I don't mind talking about speedballs pitched for old trophies while someone else carries a tray balanced by beer bottles. Those aren't Wiffle ball bats mounted on the wall, you know. Not any red rose in the snow, or computer-generated heart with starbursts next to a kitten angel mewing under its halo in the candlelight of a baby sucking an adult finger where a naked lady stares with longing eyes through two curled fingers toward the animated passion of bunnies, butterflies, and lovers beached in a valley where bashful hats bend down obscuring bow ties in a seizure of robotic choreography revelatory of no organic nature.

Dear Meaningless Existence,

You know I don't have to be there for you if I don't want to.

66 — Son

Dear Fake Advice Columnist,

I don't know how to honor my father. He died, and so
now I'm fucked because I can't ask him. Do you have any ideas
that will help me? I was hoping you could steer me towards a
bunch of objective correlatives or something: maybe
otherworldly hourglass figures with unbounded futures but
unfulfilled hopes, green macaws, birthday cake and creamy fish
net venture chase clubs, spades, hearts with hated palm trees in a
heated lawn in some little city in a big resurgent desert. What I'm
looking for here is some way where I can honor him without
having to do all the things he always told me to do. I need a way
to make myself feel really good about everything without having
to invest actual tradition in my life.

Dear Son,

Hopefully your father left you a really fancy antique car in his will. That's what you're going to need here. Yes. I see it. It's hard to say what's an integral part of who anyone is. Hand me that clapper board. And go again but with more external bravado. In your case, the burnt orange 1974 MGB that may have meant everything to two generations of men, separated forever now by an eroding clock—death, really—with its resonant second hand in the night.

11 — Rubber Band Ankles

I asked the advice of a writer. He said, "Take out the function words and work it over again." So I went to my wardrobe and ripped the legs off my pants and tore the sleeves from a thousand shirts. Practical pockets full of change, of car keys and annoyance, useless slabs of fabric freed from duty, frayed out at the edges, dropped to the floor. Take out the function. Okay. So I'm left naked wearing a bit of embroidered appliqué thinking, "This can't be right. Maybe he meant something different."

68 — Doting Daddy

Dear Fake Advice Columnist,

My wife just had her first baby, and it's obvious that she has no idea what she's doing. When I'm out on the screened-in porch getting high with my buddies we talk about how she can't even hold the thing right. I really want her not to fuck my kid up. Can you tell me how to set her straight?

Dear Doting Daddy,

Shut up! Don't bother me right now! For the love of Christ. Can't you see I'm busy? I'm staring at anxiety and dependency whipping up out of a chimney. I'm listening to a reconstructable street. There are men under the pavement, adjusting things. So if you ever want your wife to have a chance, cut her off the marketed-magazine-mothering-kryptonite. She does not need to know the effect of soft plastics leeching into liquids and forever damning unborn male genitalia.

There are no dragon kites to fly on the beach at this point. Just keep telling your wife she's doing it right, you're doing it right, that you trust both her and yourself, and I am telling you, you'll be riding down the freeway waving that child out the sunroof, letting him cut fuses short and shoot bottle rockets at the tires of passing cars in no time!

And you'd better fucking listen to this: Teak furniture under redbud trees in spring does nothing to block out the woman walking with a cane, the garbage truck, the car with its hazard flashers on parked across the sidewalk in the neighbor's driveway, the stolen stop sign, the sinkhole without an orange cone, the bus with no air-conditioning, the pedantic pedestrian response to a self-preserving cyclist on the sidewalk who doesn't give a shit what anyone thinks, the rapture (an apocryphal joke, you know), the panty lines of strangers, the one tiny scratch that will ruin a good piece of furniture, the steep loose-graveled hill-climbing ends of fire service roads in old-growth forests where lit matches should never get dropped, the bunker no one would actually build in the backyard (not for real), the broken cord on the blinds, the old toilet that uses too much water for any sensible, conscientious person of sleepless social awareness.

69 — Boys Club Relic

Dear Fake Advice Columnist,

I was hoping to buy a t-shirt that expresses my worldview. But I don't really have one. I make minimum wage right now and am living at home. I go over to my friend's house next door and help him when his truck isn't running good. Sometimes I give my buddy fifty bucks if he's out of work or something. But I don't really know what I think about everything enough to get the right t-shirt.

Dear Boys Club Relic,

My grandmother is recovering from a hip replacement. This summer she needs someone to look after her and help out with getting the mail and groceries.

71 — Calm & Collected

Dear Fake Advice Columnist,

I'm recently divorced and find myself foundering in a wash of traditions that could have meant something if marriage, family, home, love, commitment, and tradition amounted to much in my personal experience. It's Christmas Eve. We're supposed to be hanging stockings for children who were never born. Is there some way that I can keep myself from going over to my ex-husband's apartment and eviscerating him with a butcher knife?

Dear Calm & Collected,

What you want to do in this case is pack as much ancillary meaning into your life as possible. It's sort of a trick, because those huge things like marriage and children and holidays are annoyingly large meaning suckers. It's not like nutritional data, circulation, passing motorcycle cops, manganese, incidence numbers for worldwide injuries, neon green eye shadow, wrinkled silk suits, shadowboxing, sleek cars rushing through sunlit tunnels, pleated leather, plated scallops, a black calfskin sectional couch, heels on a chair back, freckles, butterfly migrations, cots and footlockers, snakeskin mini-trench coats, puppies in the mountains, pearl drop earrings on a cobblestone side street, sequin tentacles, and an updo stuffed with paper begonias. If you're not careful marriage, children, and holidays assume this disproportionate status in a life. It's easy to lose sight of all the ridiculously small areas of existence into which you can invest meaning if you are diligent and committed. For instance, you can have a shadowy figure in taxi yellow jeans invest meaning two nights a week after he guzzles a quick-down, can-by-can, six-pack, claims to have lost his cell phone, again, and arrives at your house banging on the windows and falling through the screen door.

74 — Repressive

Dear Fake Advice Columnist,

Sometimes I fantasize about sex. But I don't think I'm that good at it. It seems like you'd have to be really, really good at it to meet the cultural standard. I don't even have a ten-foot set of feathered wings. And I really have a hard time imagining slathering myself with a hot-thick layer of banana-passion body oil so I can be all self-possessed to hump two truckers and a wombat.

Dear Repressive,

You're not alone. Well. You are. But. I mean a lot of people—look, it doesn't matter. Just listen. Visualization is everything. Let's set a scene:

1) It's early. So. Get there. Get hateful and empowered.

2) It's a twin bed. Like at camp. Steel spring frame. Rusted-out joints. Everything.

3) Now. Think of other sweaty people. As many as you want. But. There's no reason to get greedy. Good. Get all worked up physically.

Take it further. Figure it out. Have any sort of sweaty successful early morning interaction with two other people in a twin bed. I know it's tough to imagine. But try. See it: Someone periodically stands up only to dive back in. That forces someone else down between the mattress and the wall, which make things impossible for whoever ends up in charge of fellatio. Don't give up. I know it sucks. Seems like a terrible cross between naked roughhousing and the most awkward cramped contrivance for sex. Let it lead to flesh dripping with sweat, covered with a salt-glistening moist heat. Good. Wait. Yeah. You're right. Let's start over. This isn't even close to the most ideal fantasy ever.

75 — Embarrassing Evidence of Societal Entropy

Dear Fake Advice Columnist,

I'm single and, okay, I'm too old to be single. Let's face it. I've got a vaginal death maw that can't be unleashed at any backyard barbecue. It scares people. Men are afraid of its becoming a trap. But worse, married women are afraid their husbands are gonna fall into it and be ripped away into the vacuum of its black hole.

So. Because of the vaginal death maw, I guess I understand why invasive control freaks who like me are always trying to set me up with these random single guys. Now. These guys aren't random to the control freaks. They're random to me. And. I'm random to them. But. The fact that these single guys are random to me and I'm random to them isn't what matters. What matters is that the invasive control freaks get to neaten up their lives and get rid of any remnant single people. It's the same as the way they put away their Christmas lights in big plastic tubs. They like order, I guess.

Anyway. So me and these random-to-me-me-random-to-them single guys are supposed to go on dates or whatever. Sometimes I guess I do putter around my apartment thinking, "Gosh, I hope utter satisfaction comes to me by means of being a pawn in someone else's desire to stave off the socially awkward moments that the threatening presence of single people creates so that my being around stops undermining their entire familial structure." Well, okay. Fine. But. Yeah. I hate dating random people and random people hate dating me.

Dear Embarrassing Evidence of Societal Entropy,

Remember that game called Memory? I love that game! My kids have a version with famous photographs of all the national parks.

37 — Celebrating a 25th Anniversary

Service culture? What are you talking about? Pull off I-65 at exit 215. Go past the Arby's, the McDonald's, the KFC, the gas station that used to be owned by the Carters and could still be. Blinker's on. Take a left. Limestone gravel parking lot. No ruts. No bumps. Always well maintained because Mr. Cover owned the Dairy Queen and he was also a contractor, as well as an eighth grade social studies teacher—all of which helped him stay in business as a small farmer in the outlying rural area around my hometown of Rensselaer, Indiana.

The Blizzard and I grew up together. My dad took me to DQ. He liked ice cream. Once in a while I'd go with the neighbor kids. We'd ride in another dad's classic Skylark, or another year in his VW punch bug with countless golf tees on the floorboards. Other times, we went as a family of four, after church, plays, band concerts, piano recitals, and honors programs. We talked and laughed with people we knew who came in talking about great steals and slides evidenced by grubby socks held up with elastic from polyester uniforms, after Little League and summer softball. Yeah, I like Dilly Bars. And, the Peanut Buster Parfait has a place in my heart. But. Please. Step aside and let me order a Reese's Pieces Blizzard, medium.

The Blizzard maker has a lot of artistic control. Or did in those days. The portions weren't specified. So. The quantity of candy was an art more than a science. So was the length of time on the Blizzard machine. I loved it when they crushed the pieces beyond recognition, which made the whole thing orange. And, other times, I loved it when the pieces were just barely chopped by some uninvested drive-thru slacker with no job security. The visored teenager haphazardly handed me something slipshod and careless, something in a blue-backgrounded waxed paper cup, something like a Reese's Pieces sundae.

Ours was the regular DQ layout. There were plaques with pictures of softball teams near the entry and smudges of ketchup on the swinging trash can door didn't last very long. The vertical glass-doored refrigerator meant for pre-made ice cream cakes later replaced a glass-covered chest of Dilly Bars. In the bathroom, there was that strange fabric loop with which to dry your hands. It replenished itself somehow. It's possible that a few giggling girls may once have stayed in the bathroom diligently trying to pull out the whole thing.

There is a misconception about the Midwestern work ethic. Probably reinforced by people like the DQ owner, with his four unrelated careers. I'm not saying that many, many people don't work very, very hard. You have to when you're poor. It's imperative. But if you are sixteen, or seventeen, or (God forbid) eighteen, there is a different brand of vigor, something less harried, something less—well, less.

At Dairy Queen, for at least twenty-five years, having a job—okay, fine, I'll go—pays for the teenage gas that you need to drive an hour to get to the movies, if that's the plan, with a date or a friend. Having a job means that for a few hours you aren't drinking beer in the backseat of a car, drag racing between the cornfields somewhere. Having a job means you aren't pregnant, just yet. Fine. These reasons to work—yours and your parents'— are a little different from working for the underwater mortgage, for the car title, for the night class, or for the kids' Little League uniforms.

I don't know if it's worse to work for the gas to drive to the movies or to be doing it for the revalued mortgage. It's hard to say. And I don't know if there is less perceivable angst in the teenager spooning glops of pineapple, hot fudge, and strawberry sauce on top of some ice cream and a broken banana or in the woman forced to take her child to work one day after learning her sitter "doesn't work bank holidays."

Because maybe the teenager just got dumped. Maybe the father of four who thinks his kid should get a job to keep him out of trouble just found out his mother is dying of something he can't comprehend. Maybe the twenty-seven-year-old is trying to find a way to pay for rent and student loans and martinis and credit card payments all at the same time. Maybe these three can't be bothered, don't have the time or patience or luxury to believe in God, in Country, in all the things that help turn "just getting by" days into diligent Midwestern work ethic days, into humble, hardworking, heaven-entry, patriotic, hellishly successive, interminable days of showing up—again—to the same place, to work.

Regardless, if you make it through the day, if you make it through the week, if you impress your mother and father, your husband or wife, with your grades, with your batting stance, with your time on the gleaner, with your driving record, with your boyfriend, with your free throw percentage, with your first paycheck, with your raise, with your contract, maybe they'll take you to DQ, for a Blizzard. Maybe they're looking for a reason to go themselves. Yes! And maybe when you get there, a paid kid behind the counter will care a little bit more than usual, will not seem put-upon or bored, will say hello, will smile, and will let you watch how carefully the soft serve goes into the medium waxed paper cup, how evenly measured the Reese's Pieces flavor morsels can be as they're spooned into the cup, how particularly the fan blade on the Blizzard machine can be lowered into the ice cream, how the switch can be turned on, and how a person (who really knows the way to make a decent Blizzard) raises and lowers the cup, in an even rhythm, with skill. How that same person turns off the fan blade, slams the cup against the counter to get rid of that central vortex, shoves a long-handled red spoon into the cup, and hands it over to you, to someone who's been watching, waiting patiently, maybe all week, maybe longer.

76 — Overwhelmed

Dear Fake Advice Columnist,

I like women. All different kinds but especially reinvented elastic driveway gate pinup girls rinsed sulfate-free. And sometimes I don't mind taking one out for a nice meal. Or for a movie or something. But then about halfway through dinner I start to freak the fuck out, you know, because no matter what, I can just sense all these overwhelming expectations she has about the situation. You know how they are with their mounting emotive tensions. If they're interested at all, you blink and they're involved. Suddenly they want to date; nay, to love; who dares to dream so small! To perish together in a bed of bliss at the end of some well-matched longevity! She doesn't know anything about who I am. So I usually just fuck her doggie style over the arm of my couch and then give her enough cash for a cab. Is there some way not to be overwhelmed by the dinner?

Dear Overwhelmed,

No.

79 — Stating the Obvious

Dear Fake Advice Columnist,

Sometimes people are assholes, pricks, bitches, and motherfuckers. Can you tell me why?

Dear Stating the Obvious,

Interactions work to keep people centered in the golden wheelbarrow on pavement iced with sweet-sixteen cadence-swung sun-damaged extremities. Everyone is always policing everyone else in these nurturing ways. When others are down, people bring them up. (That's when you like people.) When others are up, people work diligently at bringing others down. (That's when you state the obvious.) It works. Not like soluble fiber exactly. It's more unblemished by instant feedback and awe-inspiring smoky eyes blasting some unforgettable announcement: the pampering oasis of an upcoming release to beat relentlessly through a sedentary layoff that will taper, burn, float, and record surges. Helps us keep to the middle of the ridge as we walk our own paths through life. It's the grace of sustenance on a blue lagoon day for a brown woman in a bikini and knee-length cardigan.

80 — Mommy Dearest

Dear Fake Advice Columnist,

I'm a stay-at-home mom, and I hate it. It's the worst job I've ever had. I want to quit, but I'm deathly afraid of the societal judgment that I'd be forced to endure for the rest of my life.

Dear Mommy Dearest,

You know, perhaps there is a derivation of getting fired in the legal system. But the real issue is resenting that there's never a way to kick back and rake in the unemployment. Such a nuisance. Try this: be one girl with heart-shaped lips pomegranate-stained and coated with eight-hour shine fix polymers; try to chew through a dripping gold necklace. Do it a little too much until someone takes a stand, because what you want is to be laid off to avoid subjecting yourself to a lifetime of constant denigration.

81 — Slacker

Dear Fake Advice Columnist,

My motivation for everything in life has totally waned. I'm thinking about giving up. Advice?

Dear Slacker,

Picture a black woman in a white body suit. Get a bike. On the straightaways: don't stop peddling; keep the rhythm consistent and set your mind free to explore unending horizons. Snap, float, high on private thoughts like oversized cards you can throw up against the low ceiling. Then, give yourself a white woman in low-rise purple pants, with a tramp stamp. Give her a purple hat, too. Make it big and floppy. But. Let her leave the sunglasses behind. They're not forgotten. It's a choice made with violins and candy apple-sticky lips. On the bike uphill: head down, power through, use your low gears, and always remember to breathe. Stroke a fluttering magazine filled with a camera's collection. Scream no doom-boom at any close walls. This situation is not a breakdown, fully. Not a violation, at all. Let go. Get along with the woman who walks into skintight sunset-lit water. The silhouette of the fringe on her sarong proves nothing more than the woman solid-calved hiking the headlands with a farrier pack. On the downhill? Fuck it, there's nothing like descent. Keep your eyes open. Pick your feet up. Let the pedals fly. Smile. Steer the best you can. And enjoy that inimitable rush of wind on your face. The subwoofers are always there with the neon coil, flashing, reminding you to please, breathe, see, worst, need, and rock.

48 — Mother/Child

Mama, don't stop being a child yourself. Freud should have kept his mouth shut. So what if we inch out on the limbs of idealized perfection, testing each soft spot with a toe? The blame game is bullshit even if we should have money in the bank, find at least one blast-lasting job, and keep our stabilized eyes in some sort of relationship established with unwandering over the great expanse.

Motherhood lies in wait. A gorilla baby holds its mother, gripping her fur. Mary sits in my hybrid with gilt halo and child. Her palms open to the world.

82 — Judgmental

Dear Fake Advice Columnist,

I'm really negative and critical. But I don't like it when other people are. How can I pass judgment on others all the time without having it come back on me?

Dear Judgmental,

So today my dentist filled a small cavity. He was like, "You don't need the anesthetic, do you?" I was like, "Um, I guess not." But basically I was like, "Whatever, man. You tell me."

If you don't enjoy submission, you've got a problem at the dentist's. You're laid back, head in his lap, mouth open, can't talk, and he's using incredibly scary tools in your face.

Anyway, then out of nowhere he offered to sand down the chips in my teeth for free. He was like, "You want me to take care of that for you? I hate to see a pretty girl with an imperfection. My treat." I was like, "Why are you pointing out my flaws?" Then he was like, "Whatever, let me get in there with a sander." So fine. I'm game. Because, let's face it, this is the most bizarre gift ever.

A minute later I was like, "My teeth are super hot." He was like, "Oh yeah. That's the friction." Then he got his fixated perfectionist vibe on, called about three women over to commend him on his achievement of sanding my incisors so well, and also for some reason to trash talk the other dentists all these girls used to work for, because apparently those guys would never treat their patients so well.

Well. Then there was this weird silence. I didn't get it at first. But. Finally I picked up on the fact that he wanted validation from me, too. (So much for free.) But I'm like, okay, sure. "You're the best dentist who's ever pointed out flaws and sanded down teeth as a community service to pretty girls."

24 — The Status Report

Here is one way to relate to the world. You may, at any given point in time, cry your status. Picture. Picture. Song. Politico. Picture. Here are the instructions: Give status reports on a periodic basis. Not every thirty seconds. Not once a week. But. Daily, appropriately.

What is a status report? Pleasant things, seen and done. Or. Whatever! Virtually every conversation I can imagine is a status report. When friends get together the entirety of the interaction is one status report after the next. Men state their status in rather physical terms and women in rather emotional terms.

Fathers may or may not be dozing in the front room while status reports are streaming by, but they have the authority to jerk to cognizance and demand the status of anything from anyone at any time. But it is the mothers who in particular are constant harpies of micromanagement when it comes to status. They are the revisionists, the censors, who demand to not only know where your physical body is in space and time but also such a plethora of data points on the status graph that anyone can succumb to a life comprised of providing one's mother with data.

Open up your wallet, suckah! Show me some sensory spectacle of self even if gray is the given field with absolutely no contrast where one is welcome to flail and panic and hyperventilate one's way towards differentiation of some kind with blue bars—real or imagined.

Wait. No! I know! Low overhead with screen printing and cheap shirts. Do it in the basement, or wherever. I can sit for quite some time watching the sailboats on the water, watching the trees toss their bright new green leaves in the wind, while munching pistachios. But. Sometimes I do other things. I enjoy drinking myself into a stupor, driving while under the influence of whatever I can afford, sleeping with strangers, spending money I don't have, going places I've never been, and being an insufferable bitch to the people I care most about. I also like being outside on a gorgeous day.

They are doing exactly what everyone does at the mall!!

I have racked my brain trying to come up with a conversation I have had recently which is not essentially a status report. Currently worth billions, these collective status reports have risen to a sort of pinnacle of human interaction.

72 — Bother

Dear Fake Advice Columnist,

I'm real apathetic about life and don't really feel like eating. Do I have to bother?

Dear Bother,

No. Don't bother. It's all too much trouble. The flavors. The sensations. The memories. The dishes. The recycling. The trash. The traditional recipes. The years on top of years. The guilt. The ghosts. You don't need it. Having to have the oven at 400 just to honor your heritage seems not at all worth it. You can subsist on things like granola bars and serving-sized bottles of cheap wine.

83 — Poor, Benighted, Self-Centered, Bitter Soul of Vengeance

Dear Fake Advice Columnist,

I got herpes from some asshole at a frat party. I am so pissed off you have no idea. I'm definitely spreading this shit to as many dickwads as I can. Sure, I almost like some of these guys, and, okay, fine, I can't seem to get over that. At this point, I don't give a fuck about anybody but myself. So is there anything I can do to extinguish any hopeful, happy feelings that may arise while I'm destroying as many people's lives as possible?

Dear Poor Benighted Self-Centered Bitter Soul of Vengeance,

It sounds to me as if you know exactly what's best. Have a nice time!

78 — Owner of Dynasty

Dear Fake Advice Columnist,

Everyone else I know got married. I'm not married and hate the idea of another person living in my home and eating the stuff in my fridge. But I want to do something really big and showy, send great cards to everyone. How should I word the invitations for a commitment ceremony to my shar-pei, Dynasty?

Dear Owner of Dynasty,

So after a while I put on some red lipstick and walked down on the beach to watch the jugglers. Right now I'm getting a six-pack and heading over to a friend's house for dinner. I take pretty decent care of myself. And I'm really good at my job.

Wait, what was your question?

84 — Familial Run-in with Religious Hypocrisy

Dear Fake Advice Columnist,

Sometimes I get confused about right and wrong. I mean I do absolutely everything everyone tells me; I'm sure I do because I resent everyone and everything, am frustrated all the time, absolutely must be with people constantly, and have no ideas of my own. So I know I've got that part right. Okay. So. I go to church and sit next to my bratty kids who kick my shins for an hour solid with their cheap patent leather shoes. Well, last week, during the invocation, I was on my way to make ten gallons of coffee in the ancient percolator and noticed my mother making out with the hot teenage acolyte in the choir practice room. She's almost sixty-three. Shouldn't Mom have a little fun with a boy toy in her spare time?

Dear Familial Run-in with Religious Hypocrisy,

What's he look like?

86 — Should Have Gotten Knocked-Up at Fourteen

Dear Fake Advice Columnist,

I went on one date from a dating website and now I've been getting harassing phone messages from the guy for almost a year. I'm not being singled out. He seems to use telemarketer technology. But I get these horribly intimidating sound-effect voice mails. They are the worst. It's totally psychologically traumatizing. I stopped checking my voice mail in the fall because of them. I couldn't deal with it. They are weird, mainly. Like movie sound effects. The scariest one is of gunshots. It sounds like it's coming from inside a firing range. I've got the cops on it, but I was wondering what to do about procreation.

Dear Should Have Gotten Knocked-Up at Fourteen,

You think too much. Cops will get you nowhere. You need to take matters into your own hands. Look at everything that's already on your plate. It's getting ridiculous. I mean your daily to-do list is like this: 1) leave the house; 2) start dating again; 3) find a soul mate in order to fulfill all life dreams; 4) be sure all the guys who turned out not to be the soul mate aren't skulking around in your vicinity honing malicious intentions just for something to do on their days off; 5) become completely and totally paranoid about ever leaving the house again.

But moving from the general to the specific, let's get down and dirty about how to cope with this phone harassment. I suggest an M60 mounted on the hood of your Prius. Just drive past that guy's house and mow his ass down. You'll probably get the old lady watering her geraniums next door and the guy who's out front there waxing his car, but at the outset factor in that kind of minimal collateral damage. There is nothing that should be coming between you and your life plan. You are on birth control for the first fifteen years after puberty, then you come off it, and go straight to the fertility clinic. This is society and those are the rules. You can't be getting sidetracked by some idiot who wants to intimidate you, just because this culture has him completely emasculated.

87 — Book Worm

Dear Fake Advice Columnist,

I almost checked a book out at the library, but there was no one at the circulation desk. I didn't know what else to do so I just took the book and walked out of the library. But somehow the book set off those alarms at the doors. It's so ridiculous. All that does it is this magnetized metal strip. So unfair. If I'd just taken the strip out, there never would have been a problem. Well. The librarian came over and made a big thing out of it like the book was hers or something. She completely embarrassed me. Shamed me and shit, you know? But I want to go back and get more books to keep for myself. I need them to put over my fireplace because they look really good in the marble bookends I got from IKEA. How I can deactivate the sensors in the collectively-owned books so that those stupid alarms don't go off next time?

Dear Book-worm,

Who does she think she is? Incompetence has reached its tipping point. Rip the covers off and run.

39 — July Visit

Mother is in town. Chicago is as good as life gets in the middle of July. We met, as soon as I could stand it, at the new Modern Wing. The Art Institute's new twin. We stood on the walking bridge talking about literature for an hour. I did not hate her so much anymore but still hated her garish jacket. My mother looked out at the water. I looked down at the prairie flowers and gravel paths in their planned boxes in the Lurie Garden. My mother stood at the edge and leaned over. I couldn't. Couldn't stand it.

88 — Want

An isolationist alienated insular island-man joined the one-set to not be so me-too-mummy-cling marginalized. Why? Because one of the one-set went to the no kind of answer, about which so many ask. And he stood there, looking, you know? Really looking.

Hobble. Cobble. Gobble. Go.

For a moment, even to him, it seemed like maybe being one of the one-set may not even crash-test matter. No. Untrue! He was really looking. And not just to look but to find, to know, to believe, to become.

46 — Love/Pity

There are corn and cattails elsewhere. Whether or not piano eyes aspire to penetrate that stained glass Joseph at the chapel I am no witness, no more. Darkness consumes objective truths but as my hand reaches out to them, they ripple. Summer thunder, snow, and gleaming memory, but I am no witness no more, whether layered bakery rolls flake apart in church basements, even if milkweed seeds silk-drift through unmoving air—despite their anchor weight—and rise past beech groves, up into sycamore-leaved nets, or if creeks still hush dry as they season pass.

If mossy summer crawdads vacation in galvanized tubs on cement slabs still shaded by remembered peonies, then likely there a praying mantis still looks down from a leaf with reserved disapproval. My father said, "Never confuse pity and love." His advice became a litmus test for coiling tendencies that seeped in through the chinks of my life where diagnosis and judgment made worm trails through my have-to-know-it-and-why mind.

Even to this day I'd rather know if the summer auditorium curtain at the high school bike rack still gets filled up with tan kids near a place where slow continual invisible men chew limestone out of the earth, lift it by dump truck, shake it up conveyor belts, pile it high to make dust and our mini-mountains. Not knowing, I'd guess a swan has stopped for a bit, again, and is preening on the quarry lake that stands at silent capacity rain after rain.

92 — Me

Dear Fake Advice Columnist,

I want to write in to ask you something, but I don't really feel invested in my life. I feel like I'd rather watch reruns of reality TV. Maybe wait for the repo guy to come get the car I leased last year. Can you think of some questions that I might be able to write in and ask you so I can point to the entry in the paper and show it to all my friends and say, "That's from me!"

Dear Me,

If you really want to latch onto existence, then it's about savage recalcitrance against the status quo. So I guess you could ask me why the fuck I care.

93 — Fuck-up

Dear Fake Advice Columnist,

I've recently gotten sober after fucking myself up on a regular basis for a solid fifteen years. I'm wondering what to do about lack of sensual stimulation. I get sort of bored, then it's almost like I'm grounded. I hate it. I want it to stop. I'll do anything. Seriously.

Dear Fuck-up,

It's too bad you're sober. I quite enjoyed having a little nip of rye whiskey this afternoon while reviewing pages at this stainless steel table, with its brushed swirls, where my bouquet of lilacs and white tulips lies so carefully on a diagonal over a corner. I've yet to get a vase. The flowers drip every once in a while from the sopping wet purple tissue paper base. The water is pooling on the antique seat of a wooden chair next to me. But even if you didn't mention it and won't, the idea of your eating tea cake and ham after sex somehow disturbs me. I'm not quite sure why. Because, if I'm honest with myself, salt-cured meat, masticated, swallowed slow, is a perfect sort of indulgence for those most sober of individuals, such as yourself.

95 — Self Help Nightmare

Dear Fake Advice Columnist,

I'm a co-dependent enabler and I love it. For ten years Dr. Phil and Oprah have made me feel really guilty about having any self-worth at all since I derive all mine from others. I don't care what the Feminists say, Womanhood has a lot of momentum and it doesn't just stop on a dime. The patterns are really old. For me, self-abdication started very young. But as I've gotten older I've harbored more and more silent resentment and frustration. I don't know. When it's another person's turn to support me somehow it never quite happens. There's always a logical explanation. That's the part that pisses me off. Not the not having support. But. The constant explanations about why I can't have it. What can I do to evade the pressure from the narcissists who dominate my entire existence?

Dear Self-Help Nightmare,

I can't be distracted from broadcasting my overbearing influence by considerations like that. Of course you resent the world for not recognizing your needs but what can be done? Living in an emotional hell doesn't compromise "who you really are," as no one else really has access to your internal shit anyway. We're all alone. Get over it.

96 — Heretic

Dear Fake Advice Columnist,

I don't believe any of it. The only reason I go to church sometimes is to feel some continuity in my life, some sense of familiarity, some connection to my childhood, and to the space beyond death.

Dear Heretic,

It doesn't sound like you're going to be able to get your quota of a derivative God. This has to stop. Don't mess with any of that shit in the beyond. It's best to stay home. How will Santa find your stocking? You can't be at Grandma's on Christmas morning. Get your mom, or some other member of your inner circle, to sync-in with a church community so that you can show up surly twice a year. God will know you've done all you can for your spirit.

98 — Sit-Down Dinner

Dear Fake Advice Columnist,

I would love to have a party where there's an auctioneer selling off abstractions all night as you make your entrance through the foyer. He'd be on stilts and have those thirty-foot stilt pants, metallic-striped, and yellow, with flutter, flow, and wooden clicks on marble floors where spring-loaded spills get cleaned up thud-quick-quiet so he won't fall. He'd stand there, shifting his weight back and forth, lifting his feet, alternately, hunched over, making a rhythm, making a spectacle, making a left, right, left, right, left, right mockery march the way stilt walkers do, entertaining onlookers with a precarious gravity play that might maybe, yes, almost betrays its physics after all, once, no, yes, after all these galactic eras, and he'd look for the highest bidder for what can't win: philosophical theories, macroeconomies, political spheres, and many too many emotional responses well-rationed. There would be no question

about value. No low-bid contracts undermining insta-structures.
He'd be streaming. And, as the hostess, I'd pay him in advance to
have a cracked-out, verbal-solid, six-and-a-half hours of old-time
auctioneering, calling our times into high frequency question, as
treble over the deafening electronic downtempo beat, coming
from somewhere out on the lanai. But I'm wondering what kind
of table service I should have.

Dear Sit-Down Dinner,

Set a table with twenty-four place settings of your finest
china and silver. Use the good crystal. At each place setting leave
a square mirror and a small pile of cocaine. Give each little
powder pile a calligraphied place card. Prop it up there. Have
each guest introduce himself or herself to his or her neighbor on
the right by snorting a line. And, if anyone wants to meet the
persons on the left? Pass the Limoges oyster plate, where 70mm,
75mm, 80mm diaphragms are arranged as special order select
delicacies.

99 — Altruist

Dear Fake Advice Columnist,

Most of the acts of my life have been altruistic. I'm basically trying to give myself permission to make decisions that may benefit me first and foremost and other people secondarily. This is REALLY tough if you've been taught the good opposite.

I wouldn't really mind catering to the group and putting everyone else's needs first. But it doesn't really seem like I have a pack for my pack mentality. Do you know what I mean? From personal history, I've found that trying to benefit the greater good, or the familial good, or the husband good is impossible. So what's a good little altruistic self-sacrificer to do?

Dear Altruist,

Not sure why you care. But we can go there. How are you even going to offer yourself for the greater good? Consensus has been deconstructed. I'm not an altruist at all. Why would I ever want to bother to help anyone else?

55 — Pothead

Dear Fake Advice Columnist,

I've been trying to reckon my identity but can't seem to remember anything that I've figured out.

Dear Pothead,

My approach to the reclamation of identity is more involved than the IKEA standard "some assembly required."

Forget everything you've already forgotten but don't forget this:

When you build your own contraption out of spare parts from the junkyard, which I do all the time, you don't really think, "Yeah, this is definitely going to work."

Not at all. There's no warranty. No receipt. No little baggie of plastic pieces carefully counted in China. There's just you and a bunch of ideas about how it all could be.

Fine. What do you do with it?

After you rig the thing with a hope and prayer, you think, "Well, if it does work, it'll be awesome. I made it myself and got all the pieces for cheap." There's also a strong, "And I didn't get tetanus or lose a finger" component in there somewhere, too.

101 — Lonely Broken Heart

Dear Fake Advice Columnist,

I go to fancy restaurants by myself...no problem. Go to the movies by myself…no problem. Go to plays alone...fine. Go on vacation by myself...great. Ice cream. Shoe stores. Bars. Concerts. Readings. Weddings. Baby showers. Business trips. Laser treatments. Haircuts. Workouts. Appointments with the financial planner. Dinners with friends. Bed. But once every couple months I'm like, "I do not want to go to the freaking grocery store by myself ever again!"

Dear Lonely Broken Heart,

Rent a husband.

If you've got a demand? I'll make the supply. I am SO the woman to start a temp-husband service. Better yet, why not form a co-op? Let's do it! I know some pimps that buy huge quantities of Viagra from the pharmacy for their employees and clientele. I figure it's just a matter of chatting these guys up and adapting the business plan. I'll make a phone call.

Middle-aged divorced men need hookers for sex. But middle-aged divorced women need husbands-for-hire to drive them to the store for a few things and to make sure they get home okay.

Just yesterday I gave my friend a bunch of shit about playing matchmaker with me. But it must have started me thinking and then here came your question, and—bam!—eureka moment. If you want to print up Rent-a-Husband flyers and hand them out in huge crowds like they do for lost pets, that's perfect. I figure that will be the most expeditious way to find both of us a nice quiet hourly guy who likes to read the paper in his slippers.

ACKNOWLEDGMENTS

Thanks to my Facebook family for tolerant support during a lengthy exploration of warring language. Special individual thanks to Heather Dewar, Lucille Fridley, Gin Havard, Melody Layne, Tammy Servies, Brian Borre, Rayne DeVivo, Jim Gratner, Peter Hale, Jane Friedman, Reginald Gibbons, Audrey Niffennegger, Sandi Wisenberg, Miles Harvey, Aleksandar Hemon, Alan Larson, Navneet Gupta, Paul Mason, Roland LMKO Rydstrom, Terri Lee, Susan J Williams, Rob Cypher, Jenny Truppo, Crystal Neal, Sherrie Toigo, Pepper D. Smith Burkholder, Carla Sizemore, Mark Rayburn, Jamie Garcia, Guy Whitney, Todd Tue, Andrea LeVasseur, Josh Seib, Deva North, Justin North, Joe P. Said, Dorothea Duenow, Zach Duenow, Morgan Sorvillo, M.J. Sorvillo, Steve Gardiner, Sunshine Wolfe, Ed Norris, Amy Greenup, Lisa Fenner, Marna Swagert, Rod Hughes, Rebecca Huehls, Jason Hirsch, Maria Kubiak, Jennifer Wohlberg, Sam Veilleux, Mike Kasky, Virginia Wallace, Alex Philbrick, Anittah Patrick, Meg Canada Knodl, Darren Mast, Genevieve Jones, Dorothy Jones, and Andrew Groh.

ABOUT THE ON IMPULSE SERIES

*

We each have an impulse to share our experience. These four collections of short works explore storytelling from catharsis to craft. Over the course of this series Nath Jones's writing style develops from the raw, associative, tyrannic rambles of cathartic non-fiction, flash fiction, and rant in *The War is Language* and our digital domains, to the delightful rough-hewn vignettes of *2000 Deciduous Trees*, into the compact characterizations of the fictionalized tellings in *Love & Darts,* and finally toward *Acquainted with Squalor*'s fully-crafted short stories that use literary devices and narrative elements to reveal a world well-rendered. In *Radar Road: the Best of On Impulse,* Morgan Sorvillo Kiger gives us a portion to desire.

ABOUT THE AUTHOR

Nath Jones received an MFA in creative writing from Northwestern University where she was a nominee for the Best New American Voices 2010. Her publishing credits include *PANK Magazine, There Are No Rules, The Battered Suitcase,* and *Sailing World.* Her current e-book series, *On Impulse,* explores the spectrum of narrative from catharsis to craft. She lives and writes in Chicago.

www.ingramcontent.com/pod-product-compliance
Lightning Source LLC
Chambersburg PA
CBHW050353190726
48284CB00007BB/2261